From Darkness
To
Light

Larry L. Deibert

This book is a work of fiction

All names, places and events are the product
of the author's imagination, or are used
factiously.

The exceptions are the characters of Steve
and Mary Wright, used with permission. They
are the owners of The Carolina Temple Island
Inn in Wrightsville Beach, North Carolina.

Sherrl Wilhide's name is used with
permission

Laura Beck's name is used with permission

I dedicate this book to Peggy Deets Deibert; my wife, my best friend and my final reader. With your assistance, I always feel I have the best book I could possibly write. Love you, honey.

Cover Photo by Denise Blanken

Cover Art by Sara Lorenz

ACKNOWLEDGMENTS

Heartfelt thanks to the Reverend Doctor Alf Halvorson, head pastor at First Presbyterian Church, Bethlehem, Pa. for reading the manuscript and assuring me that all my religious issues work.

Thanks, Dr. Barry Slaven for assisting me with my medical questions.

Thanks, Joseph Gackenbach, my former eye doctor for assisting me with my vision questions.

Thanks, Linda Furlow-Patty for your edits and support for the third time.

Thanks, Nick Zumas for your assistance for the second time. I am honored having you as a friend.

Thanks, Laura Beck, my daughter. You always seem to pick up the who, what, when, where, how and why issues. Love you.

Thanks, Peggy Deets Deibert. Without your love, support and editing skills, my books would not be as good.

Thanks, Sara Loren, my daughter in law, for your ability to turn a photo into a great cover. Love you, DIL

Wednesday, July 9th, 2014
Wilmington, North Carolina

1

Rick Conlen sat on a bench with his girlfriend, Denise Scott by his side. He touched her arm and said, "We have company."

Denise was getting accustomed to Rick telling her that a ghost had just appeared to him. Unless the spirit chose to have others see and hear it, she would only hear Rick's conversation. She watched him nod as he listened to the spirit, and after a few moments he turned back to her.

"His name is Cecil Goodwin. He was a boilerman on the North Carolina during the war. In sixty-one, not too long after the ship was moored across the river, he was walking on this side of the river. He looked over and saw some of his buddies, who had perished onboard, wave to him. The sight scared him to death, and he's been haunting this area ever since."

"So what does he want from you?"

"Haven't gotten that far yet. I guess he'll tell me when he's ready."

A moment later, he materialized, scaring a neatly bearded, bald man, sporting rings in each ear. He was carrying a fishing rod and a white bucket; both fell from his hands. The bucket bounced and came to rest at Denise's feet. It was empty.

Regaining his composure, the man stammered, "What's going on here?" He pointed to Cecil. "He just appeared out of thin air." He saw Cecil smile.

"I'm a freaking ghost, Sonny. Now get your stuff and leave or I will haunt you forever."

The man picked up his bucket and rod and trotted away, pausing to look back once to see the spirit draw a finger across his throat.

In spite of herself, Denise had to laugh and then Rick laughed too.

When Rick turned his attention back to Cecil and Denise, he gasped. He was beginning to see her more clearly than in the past several weeks.

She saw the look on his face and said, "You okay? You look like you saw a ghost." Shaking her head at the stupidity of that, she laughed. "I think I'm losing it." She even saw Cecil smile.

"Yeah, I'm fine. I think I may have turned my head too quickly and a little pain took me by surprise." He wanted to talk longer as he studied her features, still a bit cloudy, but it sure seemed like his sight wanted to come back, and all he could hope is that when he regained full vision, if ever, he would get himself checked out.

"Good, glad to hear that you'll be okay. Cecil, can I ask why you're still earthbound?"

He smiled. "You sure are pretty, Denise. My wife was a very attractive woman. I was thirty-nine when I died. She was thirty-seven then and my death ruined her. She turned to alcohol to ease her pain and died penniless and homeless at forty-two. Fortunately, she never became earthbound and I truly hope that when I can leave this state, I will see her again." He paused, stood up and pointed to the ship. Three specters were waving to him. He looked back toward Rick and Denise. "Those are my buddies. I think I might be earthbound because I'm still connected to them and I don't know how to break free from the pull of the spirits still on the ship. They have been aboard for a long time. How can we move on, Mr. Conlen?"

Rick shrugged his shoulders. "Cecil, I'm afraid I can't answer that right now, but perhaps someday you will all be able to move on. I've been studying this subject for as long as I've had this gift of ghost whispering. I've set up a website and a Facebook page to find others like me, but no luck so far. Just hang in there and we'll see you again." He stood up and began to walk away. Denise said goodbye to Cecil and quickly caught up with Rick, slipping an arm through his.

"You were a little curt with him, Rick. What's going on, honey? That is totally not like you."

"You're right, of course. I shouldn't have taken that tone, but when I can't solve a problem, I get pretty testy." He took her hand. "Sorry, honey. I'll try to do better." When he looked at her, her face was becoming even clearer and he was amazed with the whiteness of her teeth. Her eye color was still hazy and there were gaps in her features, and he was getting anxious for that moment when he would see all of her. Last night before they made love, her naked body started to come into focus. She had an amazing figure. He was a lucky man.

She nodded. "Okay, this girl is getting a little hungry. How about we head to the Front Street Brewery. I've never eaten there but a friend told me they make killer fried green tomato BLTs. That and a couple of beers should fill me up to here." She said, raising her hand to her forehead.

When they were nearly out of sight, Cecil floated over the river, not able to go past the midway point. He saw his ghostly buddies urging him on but to no avail. He kept getting stopped by some kind of invisible wall. He took one more look at Rick and Denise and his face turned to pure evil. He screamed his unheard promise. *IF YOU DON'T FIND A WAY FOR ME TO LEAVE MY EARTHBOUND STATE AND BE ABLE TO SEE MY WIFE AGAIN, IT IS DOUBTFUL EITHER OF YOU WILL SURVIVE WHAT I WILL DO TO YOU.*

2

After being seated at a table on the second floor, Rick started looking around at all the people enjoying themselves. The sight of people smiling, having fun, eating, and drinking filled him with so much joy that he thought he would burst. Every passing hour was moving him to total sightedness and he was so excited. He wanted to tell Denise so badly, but he needed to see an optometrist first. Yesterday he called Dr. Elliot Mayotte, to explain how his sight was returning in the last three weeks. "Elliot, I don't understand what's going on, but I want to find out if regaining my eyesight will be permanent. Could you see me tomorrow?"

"Certainly, Rick. I have a full schedule, but why don't you come to my private entrance around eight and I'll give you a thorough examination."

"That would be great. I am so anxious to tell Denise that I'm regaining my sight, but I need to be certain that the change is permanent."

"Okay, I'll check you out. See you tomorrow."

Elliot hung up the phone before he had a chance to say goodbye. He was one of the best in North Carolina, and if he couldn't give a clean bill of eye health, nobody could.

Moments after he filed that thought, a young lady, Katrina, came to the table and asked if they wanted drinks. Rick came within a nanosecond of reaching for the menu, when Denise pointed to her eyes and then at him, nearly causing him to laugh. Katrina nodded, a sad look falling over her face. "Rick, how would you like a Battleship Pacific Pale Ale. A buck from each beer goes to help defray maintenance expenses for the North Carolina."

"That would be great."

Denise said, "I'll have the same, Katrina."

As they waited for their drinks, she talked like a magpie, but Rick only listened half-heartedly. He was too interested in people watching.

He was truly astounded with the assortment of hairstyles, clothing choices and footwear in one place. Two guys, whom he thought might be gay, since they were holding hands, were dressed in outlandish t-shirts with provocative graphics silk-screened on them. One wore sandals with white socks and the other wore well broken in work shoes and knee socks with little hearts on them. Both of them wore expensive looking sunglasses and their haircuts were perfect. He had to hold his astonishment inside, but it was getting harder to do.

Katrina brought their beers and then took their orders. While Denise fiddled with her iPhone, Rick went back to people watching. Young couples were enjoying a variety of foods, the scents filling the space with wonderful aromas. He hoped he would retain this heightened sense because most times the odors were pleasant. A trio came in. The gentleman sported a well-trimmed white beard and his head was covered with a black ball cap sporting the words VIETNAM VETERAN AND PROUD OF IT. Since Denise wasn't paying any attention to him, Rick lifted his glass and nodded to the man, recognizing his service to the country. He was with two women, casually, but elegantly dressed in designer tops. Both of the women were laughing and talking and wearing matching wide-brimmed hats. He thought they looked quite lovely and were aging slowly. He couldn't figure out why the man was with two women, but that was probably good fortune for him. After they were seated at the next table, he overheard their conversation with Katrina. The husband and wife stayed in Wrightsville Beach last year and decided to come again and bring her best friend. The man said, "I like this deal because they can go shopping and I can play golf several times this year."

The restaurant was steadily filling up and there wasn't an empty seat at the bar. He could see that some of the windows of buildings across the street were being tinted red; the sun was beginning to set. The sight was so wonderful and he couldn't wait until he and Denise could enjoy a sunset together.

An hour later, after several drinks and really good food, they left the Brewery and walked around the riverfront a little bit before hopping in the car and returning home to Southport.

It had been a good day and they were both very tired. He hoped he would be able to get some sleep but he was so excited to find out if his regained sight would be permanent.

Thursday, July 10th, 2014
Southport, North Carolina
Wrightsville Beach, North Carolina

1

Elliot Mayotte sat at his desk and after placing stereo headphones over his ears, he turned on the mini tape recorder he had pulled out of the top drawer. He turned it on and listened to Rick's words of ten weeks ago when they met face to face.

"Doctor Mayotte, as I told you yesterday on the phone, I've been blind since the age of fourteen. I tumbled down a hill while skiing and hit my head on a rock. What I didn't tell you, or anyone, as a matter of fact, was that just before I fell, I saw a pinpoint of bright, white light, the brightest light I've ever seen and I was mesmerized. The faster I skied down the hill, the closer and larger the light grew until it took on the shape of a door." He paused for several moments and then after a deep breath, he continued. "I looked through the light and saw my grandfather, who had passed on when I was nine. It appeared as though he was waving to me, until I realized he was working his hands in a pushing motion, waving me away instead of in. Doctor Mayotte, I have never felt such at peace, and I thought God was ready for me."

As he listened to the tape, Elliot jotted down notes on a legal pad. *Lunacy or reality? Did he really see his dead grandfather?*

"My grandfather appeared to try to vigorously push me away from the light. I knew I wasn't ready to join him and others I could see. One of the people, for lack of a better term, I saw was dressed in Confederate gray. He had a dirty, bloody bandage wrapped around his head and his left eye. His uniform was in tatters and his left leg was gone, just above the knee. He must have been so afraid when he died because his eye was open so wide. His mouth was open as though he was screaming. It chilled me to the bone, Doc."

Elliot scribbled furiously. *Why would he claim to have seen a dead Confederate soldier? Some connection with his family?*

"With each passing second, the door loomed larger and I feared I would pass right though it and disappear from the face of the earth. I couldn't leave my family like that, so I bent my knees and leaned all the way to the left until I felt my weight lifting my skis off the ground and I began to tumble. I prayed that I would not die today and asked God to forgive my sins and allow me to continue his work here on earth, whatever he wanted me to do."

Elliot turned off the tape player and put down his pen. He would write no more because he was a man of faith and he believed that God had a plan for all of us, even though he still couldn't understand why good people died young and some of the worst people kept on living, murdering, raping, and stealing. He figured that someday when he was in heaven, all his questions could be answered. He turned the player back on and listened to more.

"I felt myself tumbling down the hill, seeing the boulder, no longer snow covered, five feet away. I steeled myself for impact, trying to turn my head away from the stone, hoping I would survive. When I hit it, I lost consciousness. Two days later, I awakened and I saw someone at the foot of my bed. He was dressed in clothing from the early twentieth century. He told me he was an earthbound spirit, who had not yet been able to find his way to the afterlife. I swiveled my head from side to side and only saw blackness, yet he came through so clearly. I didn't know what I was supposed to do, but after he told me how he died, he disappeared from my sight, I went back to the darkness that would be the rest of my life, I thought."

"I never told anyone about him, nor the many spirits that have found me during my lifetime. Once they told me how they died, or the major sin they committed, that kept them earthbound, they would disappear. During these interventions, I kept believing that my sight was coming back, because I am now at the point where I can see shadows. Do you think my sight could be returning?"

Elliot had no idea what to expect when Rick arrived, especially after seeing him a couple of times, not finding anything that would lead him to believe that Rick would ever see more than shadows, if he was indeed seeing anything at all. He heard a knock on the door and he answered it.

"Good morning Rick."

"Morning, Elliot. You look great except for that little spot of creamer on the left side of your mouth."

Elliot turned toward the mirror on the wall and saw the creamer. He turned back to Rick. "I don't know how you are able to see and I'm going to examine your eyes to see if there is any medical reason why your sight is returning. There are cases of temporary blindness that have been resolved, but you've been blind for such a long time, I honestly can't see that happening. Let's step into an examining room.

Rick walked to the room and sat down in the exam chair. Elliot sat down on a stool immediately in front of him.

"First, I want to check your visual acuity with a series of hand and light movement tests."

He held fingers up and Rick responded with the correct number. Then Elliot moved the finger test to see how much peripheral vison he had. Once this was determined, he held up fingers on both sides of Rick's face, and again the patient responded correctly every time.

Next, Elliot moved a small penlight around, having Rick follow it with his eyes. Rick's eye muscles and cranial nerves seemed to be fine. He checked his pupils by moving the light different distances from his eyes, noting how the pupils reacted it. Rick passed this test with flying colors.

"Okay, Rick. Now I'm going to instill some anesthetic drops to measure the pressure in your eyes. Then I'll put in dilation drops to see into the back of your eyes." His pressure was very good and Elliot could not see any damage to the retina.

"This is truly amazing, Rick. In my experience with head trauma, total blindness is not very common.

Generally a blow to the head that severe would cause death instead. I think the next thing I should do is diagnose your optic nerve. It is possible that if your visual cortex is intact, you could possibly have 'seen' things recorded in your visual memory." He still didn't understand why Rick saw the Confederate soldier and that would probably puzzle him for some time to come.

When he performed the test for optic nerve damage, he looked several times, not believing what he was seeing. The optic nerve was severed and Rick should not be able to see anything. He was truly puzzled. He heard a noise in the outer office and excused himself to see what the devil it was.

Elliot opened the door to the reception area and saw a young girl sprouting wings, a Confederate soldier and an old man. He smiled believing that Rick had regained his vision through Divine intervention and no exam in the world would ever change that result. He nodded at the specters and stepped back into the exam room.

"Everything okay?" Rick asked.

Elliot smiled. "Everything is marvelous. I think you will have your sight for many years to come because you passed every test I gave you. Congratulations."

Rick stood up and shook Elliot's hand. "Hope I don't have to see you anytime soon for another exam."

The specters stood behind Rick, allowing Elliot to see them again. "Yeah, me too."

2

After his appointment with Elliot, Rick returned to the office. Denise was at her desk feverously working on a ten inch high stack of letters. She had removed them all from their envelopes and Rick watched her at work. She picked up a letter, quickly read it and then typed a response on a word document. She finally noticed him standing there and swiveled her chair.

"So where have *you* been while I've been at my desk working my fingers to the bone while you're out lollygagging somewhere, not telling me. What's the deal, Conlen? Playing blind man's bluff in the traffic?" She rambled on a little bit longer and then said, "Why the hell are you smiling, Rick? I worry about you when you go out and don't tell me where you're going."

"That's a beautiful yellow sundress you're wearing. The color looks so good next to your tan, and I must add, very long legs. I love the way you styled your hair, and your eyes are sooo green! I don't think I've ever seen a more beautiful woman than you. I think I'm going to have to marry you someday."

She sat there with her mouth wide open, not knowing what to say. A moment later she understood. He was able to see her. She jumped up from the chair, rushed toward him and kissed him hard. "How?"

"I don't understand how, but I think each time I saw a ghost, my sight returned a little bit more. I could see everything yesterday when we were out. Full vision returned after seeing Cecil, but I wanted
to see Elliot this morning. He assured me that he saw nothing that would cause me to become blind again. He thinks I will be able to see for the rest of my life."

"Honey, that is wonderful. I loved you when you were blind, but now that you can see…." She sobbed a little and then smiled. "I guess I'll love you even more, especially since you'll be able to drive for a change."

He laughed so hard he thought he wouldn't be able to stop. When he did, he said, "Really! And what will I use for a driver's license?"

She nodded. "Didn't think of that. I guess we'll have to get you a learner's permit and teach you how to drive."

"I guess we'll have to go get me a license and then you can teach me to drive. Do you know where to pick one up?"

She grabbed her purse, passed him and flipped the closed sign on the door. She held the door open and then turned around to see he was still just standing there. "While we're young, Conlen. Let's move."

When they strolled out toward her car, Rick noticed a little girl staring at them from the other side of the street. She waved to him but he didn't know if he knew her or not. Perhaps she was the child of a client, but he really didn't think so. He figured he'd remember her eventually.

Denise pulled out a little too quickly and was rewarded by the screeching of brakes, a blaring horn and the international symbol of love being thrown by the driver of a cherry red classic Camaro. She had seen the car before and she thought it belonged to a frequent patron of The Pharmacy. Once she put her finger on it, she'd give him a piece of her mind even though she was the one who screwed up. As he was passing by, she yelled, "Kiss my ass."

Rick was snickering. "And you're going to teach me to drive. That ought to go over real well."

Denise shot him a look, and then went back to driving. After she settled down for a couple of minutes, she said, "I'm sorry I acted like that, Rick. I'm just so happy for you and excited that soon you will be driving."

A few minutes later they pulled in front of the Southport DMV office but it was closed.

"So what do we do now, Denise?"

She was already dialing the number listed on the front of the building. After listening for a few moments, she dialed another number. She put her phone on speaker mode and soon someone answered. "Shallotte DMV, Examiner McMillan speaking."

"HI. My name is Denise Scott. I have a friend with me who needs to get a driver's license. We live in Southport and this is the number I was given to call. What do we have to do?"

"Well, first of all, does your friend have a car and insurance? He'll need both to take his driving test."

Rick grabbed the phone. "Hi, Miss. My name is Rick Conlen...."

"Are you the man who helped solve the mystery of that sailor who went missing on the North Carolina in World War Two?

"Yes, ma'am. That's me."

"But you're blind. You can't get a license if you're blind." Her voice was much louder now and very stern.

"I know that, but my sight has returned and I was told I will not go blind again."

"Well, bless my soul, young man that is wonderful news. You can certainly drive in that case."

"Thanks. I don't have a car nor insurance, because I never thought I'd be able to drive, but it shouldn't take too long to get them. What would I then do to get my license?"

"Mr. Conlen, all you would have to do then is come to our office and fill out some paperwork. It will take seven to ten days before you receive it, but you can get a temporary license and begin to drive immediately after you take an exam on the computer."

"What kind of questions will there be?"

"The test covers pretty much everything that a driver needs to know. When you are here, you can take practice tests, and I imagine you can find some online as well."

"Thanks, Miss McMillan. You have been very helpful. I'm sure we'll be seeing you soon."

"I look forward to it. But, don't bring any ghosts with you, please." She laughed then.

"I'll try not to, but you never know. Take care."

He handed the phone back to Denise. "Bye, Miss McMillian. Thanks for helping us."

"You are very welcome, Miss Scott. See you soon."

After Denise put her phone back in her purse, she said, "That's a bummer. Guess I'll be your chauffeur for a little while longer. The pay is pretty good though." She squeezed his butt. "So what should we do now?"

"Well, a friend of mine owns a condo in Wrightsville Beach. I don't think he'll be down for another week or two. Maybe we could go there for a long weekend."

"That would be wonderful." She pulled out her phone. "What's his number?"

3

They had gone back to Rick's office. He walked to his desk and she took the stairs two at a time to the apartment on the second floor. She moved in a week ago. She first saw him a little less than a month ago, He was seated at one of the wrought iron tables straddling the front door at

The Pharmacy. She was a bartender there and after a couple stiffed her, she took off after them. They literally disappeared. It was the first time she had ever seen ghosts, not knowing that until sometime later that day. The young couple she had served dropped their bottles and that was when she noticed that they were no longer in the restaurant.

A little later she brought Rick a beer and after sitting down at the table she discovered that he was blind. She never put two and two together, not realizing that his dog, Riley, was a seeing-eye dog. She had a feeling she was falling in love with both Rick and Riley at that moment, but she was never one to jump into relationships too quickly.

She packed clothes for both of them, grabbed a couple of towels, their toiletries, her hair dryer and styling wand, tossing everything into a soft overnight bag. When she came back down the stairs, she saw Rick on the phone and he was also going through some of the mail she had laid out to answer. She headed to the kitchen to grab a couple of bottles of water, a bag of popcorn, a plastic jar of roasted peanuts and three Cadbury candy bars. When she was finished, she took the bag of snacks and water into the office and set them down beside the overnight bag. Rick was tremendously engrossed in reading a letter and his coloring drained from his face. She thought it might be bad news, but she didn't recall any of the letters coming from a family member or a close friend. They all appeared to be 'fan letters' of a sort.

When he finished reading, he had tears in his eyes. He stood up, walked over to her and handed her the letter.

Denise took it in her hands, she had never felt paper like this before. It was unbelievably thin and was the purest white she had ever seen. So white that when she finally looked at the words, written in perfect calligraphy, the intensity of the paper momentarily blinded her and took her breath away.

Dear Rick and Denise,

My name is Hannah Sullivan. Rick saw me this morning when I was standing across the   street from his office. I know he was trying to figure out how he knew me and I think he began to understand once he started reading this letter.

I died at the age of ten from a severe case of meningitis. My death devastated my parents and my two brothers and one sister. All three were several years older than me and quite often it seemed as though I had five parents because I was ill from the time I was born.

Frequently I wished they would just be my siblings, but those kinds of joys were few and far between.

I was born in 1874 in Janeway, Wisconsin. My folks never had much and our farm was the   only   thing that kept us all going. Sometimes the crops were meager and we had to tighten   our bellies, but God provided all we needed during the lean times.

After I died, God sent me back to earth many times to assist earthbound souls. I guided a   good many to heaven, but Satan took his fair share as well. It was always heartbreaking to see a spirit descend, soundless screams coming from their mouths. I still ache for some.

There are many earthbound souls still, so God sent me here to assist you as you guide them   to   the afterlife. The Gathering will occur before month's end and you two will need all your strength to do His work. I will be with you to offer the knowledge and abilities that I possess.

He wants you to enjoy your weekend in Wrightsville, but before you return home, you are going to be witness to some marvelous occurrences.

I will meet you on Monday. I don't have to tell you when and where because you will know; actually, by that time, both of you will know, as Denise has also been charged by God for this mission.

Until then, may God's love shine down on you and give you peace.

Hannah

Denise nearly dropped the letter, her hands were shaking badly. She looked at Rick and saw he was still weeping. She waited a few moments for him to regain his composure. "Rick," she called softly. When he lifted his head, she saw his eyes were so red and swollen from the tears he had shed. "This is amazing and fearful at the same time. I have never been much of a church goer. Why would God want me to participate in The Gathering and what will happen after that? Is the end of the world at hand?"

Denise shrugged her shoulders. "Reading that letter really shook you up. I know it was intense but I can't understand why you broke down. Can you please tell me, honey?"

"When I saw Hannah earlier, I knew I had met her before, and while I read the letter, it all came back to me. Most of my tears were tears of joy. After I began tumbling down that hill, and looked up to see the boulder looming larger and larger, knowing I was going to hit it, I saw Hannah. She was only there for a brief moment, but I have never forgotten her face. Perhaps I didn't recognize her immediately because I was so pumped up from regaining my sight and that was the only thing running through my mind."

He stood up and began to pace. She just watched and listened.

He turned toward her. "She had the most angelic face. The sunlight danced on her well brushed, light brown hair Her face had a golden glow to it, much like someone who spent time in the sun at the beach. She had the most beautiful blue eyes I had ever seen. She smiled at me and said, 'We will meet again.' After I regained consciousness, she was on my mind, but I didn't tell anyone because they probably would have thought me crazy.

"I don't think the end of the world is in sight, but I think God wants all his spirits gathered and sent to their final reward, to clear the path for living humans. I had always read that when the Rapture occurs, all the dead would rise. Perhaps God is going to allow people to see these spirits leave earth to give us all time to change our ways. All I know is, I will do whatever He wants me to do and Hannah told us to have some fun, so let's get going."

She was somewhat shocked by his complete turnaround, but she loved him and would follow him anywhere. She nodded and smiled. They locked up the office, jumped in the car and were on their way to Wrightsville Beach.

4

On the way, they stopped at Harris Teeter to purchase groceries, beer and wine. They planned on having breakfast out on Saturday and Sunday, but Rick was going to make eggs and bacon tomorrow morning. Sandwiches were on tap for Saturday and Sunday.

Denise pulled into the parking lot of the Surf Suites Motel. They took the elevator to the fourth floor and when Rick opened the door of his friend's condo, he smiled from ear to ear.

Denise loved it. The condo was large with two bedrooms, the master bedroom featured a wall mounted 40 inch flat screen TV. There was a large closet and a private bath. The second bedroom was smaller but it was a comfortable looking guest room. The living room and dining room were combined. Denise loved the fireplace and if they ever had an opportunity to get this place in fall or winter, she would enjoy a roaring fire. The kitchen was large enough for two or more people to work in. Rick opened the sliding glass door and stepped out onto the balcony. He looked up and down the beach, seeing a great many men, women and children enjoying themselves. Scores of people were bobbing up and down in the water, which looked very inviting. A couple of kids and adults were body surfing or balancing on boogie boards, riding the waves. In the distance, there were about twenty sailboats riding the ocean. He actually saw a dolphin jump, and as it momentarily hung suspended above the water, Denise joined him on the balcony and saw it too.

He slapped her butt. "Last one on the beach buys dinner." He laughed as he raced toward his suitcase on the bed, with her in hot pursuit.

They quickly changed and hurried down to the beach. Denise planted her flag-her chair-first and claimed victory. Rick was only a few seconds behind, but he knew he was beat.

"I heard about a great hot dog stand on the other side of the drawbridge. I guess that would be a good place to eat,' she said, playfully.

She threw a handful of sand at him and then laughed. "C'mon, Conlen, put some sunblock on my back, so we can get into that water. It looks so inviting."

They both applied generous amounts of sunscreen to all the exposed parts of their bodies and ran to the water's edge. He grabbed her hand and they took off struggling through the water until they were far enough in to go under.

While swimming underwater, pulling himself with tremendous arm and leg strength, he had his eyes open and they grew large when he saw a ghost swimming right under him, face up. The spirit smiled and nodded his head. Rick was so taken by surprise, he opened his mouth and was rewarded with the rush of seawater across his tongue and down his throat. He quickly rose to the surface, only five feet above him. After he broke the surface, he coughed up water as he took in a few good breaths of fresh air.

A moment later, Denise broke the surface beside him, seeing him struggle with his breathing. She grabbed him around the waist to keep him up because he appeared to be heading back under. When she had him stabilized, she stroked his cheek and asked, "Are you okay?"

He nodded and started treading water. "Yeah, I guess I opened my mouth and swallowed a whole bunch of seawater. Salty as hell."

"So why would you open your mouth under water?"

They were at a point where they could both stand. "A ghost was swimming beneath me, face up and it really caught me by surprise. It was a man. He was slender and tall. He was wearing a uniform of sorts. I think the style was from the late 1800s or early 1900s. I'll have to Google uniforms. He smiled and nodded his head and then just vanished. I think he moved on to the afterlife, because I felt him touch me before he disappeared."

They stepped out of the water and went to their chairs. Rick grabbed a bottle of water from the beach bag and took a couple of deep swallows and then rinsed his mouth.

She was drying her hair, staring at him. "I think we're going to have a lot of ghostly visits before The Gathering. It seems as though we will have a pretty important role in God's plan. I'm ready for it, but like Hannah said, let's have a lot of fun until we see her on Monday," she said, smiling brightly. Inside though, she felt slightly ill, probably because of the anxiety of what they might have to do.

5

After a short session of lovemaking and a shower, they dressed casually in shorts and t-shirts, and then walked to the Oceanic for dinner. They were able to get seats on the pier and had the good fortune of little wind. Nothing would blow around and the food would stay hotter longer.

Their server, Kaylin, brought them drinks. He had a Yuengling lager and she chose a Parrot Bay Mayhem as her cocktail.

For appetizers they decided to share sunburned shrimp and a Caesar salad. For their entrée, they both chose the Oceanic mixed grill. When Kaylin walked away, they began drinking.

"Rick, this place is really nice. If we ever come here again, I could certainly have dinner here once or twice."

"Yeah, me too." He stared out toward the ocean, seeing several parasurfers gliding through the air, back down toward the water. He noticed a woman standing by the railing. She looked oddly out of place in a long dress with a shawl wrapped around her shoulders. She was wearing a large hat festooned with what appeared to be real flowers, but today's silks fooled him more than once. She was wearing gloves and held a tiny purse in her left hand. In her right, she carried a parasol. When she turned toward him, half of her face was gone and her dress was torn to shreds. Blood was dripping from her arms, legs and her chest. A knife was sticking in her chest. She mouthed the words, "Help me, Rick. I want to leave this place."

Denise noticed her too, and she could also read her lips. She touched Rick's arm, shook her head and then got up. She walked toward the woman and laid her hand on the woman's gory face and smiled. The woman nodded and said, "Bless you, child." She vanished.

When Denise returned to the table, she said, "I think we are going to be very busy for quite a long time."

He simply nodded and smiled.

6

After dinner and two more drinks, they started walking back to the hotel. As they approached an old two story building with a wrap-around porch, they heard music; a guitar and a fiddle. The music drew them to the back steps where they saw a man and a woman sitting on director chairs playing and singing an old Irish tune. After the song ended, the couple was rewarded with hand claps. Rick and Denise also clapped.

The woman, who was playing the fiddle, motioned them to step on the porch with her bow.

They stepped on the porch and were greeted by a man sporting white hair and a neatly trimmed white beard. Beside him stood a nice looking woman with black hair. The man said, "My name is Steve Wright and this is my wife, Mary. Welcome to the back porch of the Carolina Temple Island Inn. We are the owners." His eyes danced and he then added, "Mr. Conlen it is a pleasure to meet you." He looked toward Denise and said, "You as well, Miss Scott. I recognized you from your pictures in the paper last month."

He invited them to sit down on a wooden swing, which they did, and they were treated to some wonderful music for the next half hour.

After the couple went inside the building and stepped into their room, Steve said, "Would you like something to drink."

"I'd like a beer," Rick said.

"Water is fine for me." Denise replied.

When Mary went inside to get the drinks, Steve said, "I guess you both saw the four guests sitting on the rockers behind Henry and Linda, our two musicians."

"I did," Rick answered and he looked toward Denise, who nodded.

"Ever since the Pederson's stayed here last month, I've followed the story pretty closely. The only thing I don't understand is that you, Rick, don't seem to be blind."

Rick explained what had happened and Steve said, "God certainly works in mysterious ways, doesn't he."

Mary stepped out on the porch, drinks in hand and said, "Yes, He certainly does perform many miracles. Steve has been talking about you two for several weeks and he was going to call you to see if you would like to visit with us after Labor Day. We are booked solid for the summer and it is keeping us pretty busy."

"I know I'd love to stay here. It is such a charming space, and you provide ghosts for us as well," Denise replied.

Rick shook his head and laughed. "Yeah, I'd like that too. I don't know at this time what our situation will be in September, but if we are free we will definitely take you up on your offer."

"I've seen several ghosts in my lifetime, but what I think we are going to shortly witness is mind boggling. I'm thinking that every single earthbound spirit is going to work its way down here sometime in the very near future. What I've witnessed in the past several weeks has been remarkable. Once this event, The Gathering, happens, we might be in store for a rough ride."

Rick and Denise looked at each other, wondering how Steve could possibly know about The Gathering, when they only were given that information this morning. Their shock must have been evident because Steve said, "I know a lot more than people think."

The Wrights stood up, and without another word, left Rick and Denise on the porch with the four spirits, who were just waiting to be sent to the afterlife.

Friday, July 11th, 2014
Various Locations

Wrightsville Beach, North Carolina

1a

After a fitful night's sleep, Rick awakened, soaked in his sweat. The room temperature was a comfortable 70 degrees, but last evening's events kept playing through his mind.

When they were left alone on the porch with the four spirits, neither he nor Denise wanted to immediately send them to the afterlife. They were hoping to communicate with the long dead spirits, three men and a woman, all appearing to be in their late 20s or early 30s. Their mode of dress suggested that they had perished in the 1920s.

Rick got up from the swing and slowly walked toward them. As he approached, one male spirit literally threw himself toward Rick, reaching out wanting to be touched. He fell short of his goal by a foot and silently crashed to the wooden floor, kicking up some dust. Had this been a silent movie, it probably would have been quite funny, but to the spirits it was serious business. After being earthbound for ninety or more years, they were absolutely ready to move on.

When the ghost pulled himself from the floor and stood up, Rick said, "Please sit down, so we can talk. Is there any way we will be able to hear what you say, or must we read lips?"

The ghosts spoke silently among themselves and after a few minutes, the one who had fallen, turned back toward Rick and Denise. He spoke in a voice that seemed to come from another place because the sound was audible but far away and very soft. "What would you like to know before we can finally leave this earth?"

Denise figured she would let Rick continue with the questions. She took her iPhone from her purse, turned it on, selected video, and placed it in front of her, aimed toward the spirits. She doubted she would capture anything, but it sure couldn't hurt to try.

"Were you all together when you died?"

One of the men, dressed resplendently in a checkerboard pattern suit, large bowtie, and a bowler hat, wearing two-tone black and white shoes nodded. "My brother, sister and I left a party in Manhattan. We all got into my brand new 1927 Packard and decided to go to another party in Brooklyn. I guess I was driving a bit too fast and Officer Morris pulled us over. He pointed to a policeman in full uniform, still carrying his Billy club and revolver. He tipped his cap and smiled.

"Officer Morris pulled us over in a deserted area of town and after we were stopped, he turned off his siren and lights and came over to the car, to my side window. He asked for my driver's license and I handed it to him, wanting no trouble."

The sister then took over the conversation. "My name is Matilda Pruitt. My brothers are James, who just spoke to you, and Henry. Henry is mute so he won't be contributing to this conversation. When Officer Morris was seated in his car, three men rushed from the shadows between two buildings with weapons in their hands. I assumed that we were going to be robbed, adding insult to injury."

She stopped talking and Officer Morris shifted on his rocking chair, seemingly preparing to continue the story.

"I was sitting in my patrol car, with the driver's door open, writing a ticket, when I was knocked unconscious. Later I found I was in a dank, dark place, a basement perhaps, along with these three. A couple of hours later, three men came into the space and started yelling and screaming at them." He pointed to the three spirits, who had their heads down. "It had something to do with some stolen items and, from what I gathered, an awful lot of money. Each of them was taken to another place and I could hear screaming for a long time. When it stopped, they came in and strangled me. I guess they didn't want any witnesses."

They became silent again so Rick gave them some time to themselves. Seemed a little weird, since they were ghosts, but he wanted to see if he could get any more information about what was to occur soon.

"Why are you on this porch, when you died in New York?"

James said, "Good question. All of us have been earthbound for so long, but we never left Manhattan. In fact, most of the time we only haunted the area where we were killed. I don't think any of us know how we actually got here, because we were in New York and an instant later we were sitting on this porch."

"Okay, I'll buy that," Rick said. "Do you know anything about The Gathering?"

Matilda answered. "We've been hearing about it for some time now. News travels fast in the spirit world. We heard all about a blind man who could see us and that when he was given sight, our earthbound days were near an end."

"Have I been given this power by God?"

The four spirits all nodded. James said, "The power has also been given to Denise, but she knows this because she has already used it, earlier at the restaurant. That poor woman looked awful. God has plans for the both of you, even after The Gathering. That is all we can tell you and now we ask that you send us to wherever God has chosen for us to go."

They stood up and floated toward Rick and Denise. The couple each touched two spirits and were pleasantly surprised to see them all spiral upward, their faces filled with joy.

After they were gone, Denise said, "I tried to shoot a video of them, but all that came out were shadows. Their voices came through but they all sounded like they had mouths full of sand and water, every word was garbled and nobody would be able to understand what was said. So we have no proof, Rick."

He replied, "I don't think we need that proof. I have a feeling that everyone in the country, no, the world will probably know of this phenomenon in the very near future."

"I used my iPad and Googled them. The brothers and sisters were involved in a great many robberies and they also were embezzlers. A lot of people lost everything because of them. Officer Morris had a clean record, until his locker was cleaned out. He had thousands of dollars stashed away and after checking out some of the people in his patrol area, it was found that he was paid for favors, looking the other way when certain criminals had plans in the works. Looks like God wanted them with Him."

"Like Mary said, "He works in mysterious ways, indeed. Guess we better get some shuteye. It could be quite busy for us over the next, days, weeks, perhaps years."

They walked back to the condo, hand in hand, undressed and silently slipped into bed. Sleep came in minutes, but it was not restful.

1b

Rick got up from the bed and looked at Denise. She was sleeping soundly and he didn't want to wake her. He grabbed a pair of shorts and a t-shirt, picked up his running sneakers and strolled out to the kitchen. The coffee was ready; he had set the timer before they went out to eat last night. Black, strong and hot, the liquid slid down his throat, sending caffeine throughout him, jarring him more awake. He gulped down two cups and noticed the sun was still below the horizon, but, by the time he hit the drawbridge two and a half miles away, it would be popping up, warming him. His mission was plaguing him, not knowing how long he and Denise would be doing whatever God wanted them to do. He figured The Gathering would be held somewhere nearby, perhaps in a large, open space, but his assumptions could prove wrong. He shrugged his shoulders and headed down to the street.

Running always made him feel really good, but he saw traffic was backing up. He thought this pretty odd because generally there were not too many cars on the road at this time of day in beach towns. Less than a mile from the drawbridge, people were getting out of their cars and trucks and making a beeline for the drawbridge. Rick ran a little bit faster, passing people who were cheering. Several even slapped him on the back as he passed.

When he arrived at the drawbridge, a hundred or more people were lined up on both sides and both eastbound and westbound traffic stopped just short of the bridge. He stopped running and started to walk, stopping in the middle of the bridge. Everyone was pointing to his right and he was amazed by what he saw. He took out his iPhone and called Denise.

Hellertown, Pennsylvania

Sixty year old Mack Trucks retiree Aaron Pammer awakened about the same time Rick was calling Denise. He thought he heard a commotion downstairs. The sounds of pots and pans clanging against each other convinced him that someone was in the kitchen. If there was an intruder in his home, he was certainly glad that his wife, Cynthia, was out of town on a business trip. She made dolls in the basement. Much like Byers Choice carolers, she dressed her dolls in handmade clothing, depicting many eras in the country's timeline. If the investors she was meeting with came up with the financing, representing forty-nine percent of the company she was creating, they would be set for life, never having to worry about money problems again. Even though he had made really good money with his hourly pay, lots of overtime in forty-one years and very inexpensive health insurance, he didn't have much to show for it. Both of them were big spenders. Cynthia loved clothing and travel and Aaron loved to play Texas Holdem for big money. He lost more than he won. They also had bought a huge home fifteen years ago and they were just able to keep up with the mortgage and other expenses of being home owners.

He opened the nightstand drawer and took out his .45 caliber handgun. It was already loaded and cocked. He only needed to take it off safety and it was ready to go. Silently he got out of bed and stealthily sauntered down the hall and stairs, happy that they had recently put in new carpeting. He continued hearing the loud noises from the kitchen, wondering why intruders would even consider making all that noise, knowing it would probably waken everyone in the house. Fortunately, their daughter and her two teenage children left yesterday, shortly before he took Cyndy to the airport. If shots were going to be fired, he was glad he was the only one there.

When he stepped off the last stair, he stopped in his tracks, listening to the sounds in the kitchen, noticing they had lessened. He padded across the living room floor and keeping low, peered around the corner of the wall into the kitchen. What he saw frightened him more than any intruder with a gun could ever frighten him.

The early morning sunlight filtered through the windows, showing him the impossibility of what he was seeing. He lowered his weapon, stood up, and gaped at the sight.

Every cabinet door and all drawers were open. The tea kettle and coffee maker were cooking away, although no heat was coming from the gas range and the coffee maker was not plugged in. The contents of the refrigerator were placed around the interior perimeter of the room. Utensils were mysteriously affixed to the cabinet doors.

Aaron quickly raced back upstairs to get his iPhone. He needed visual proof of all this so nobody would think he had lost his mind. He hurried back down and once again went into the kitchen. When he got there, something new had happened. In the few minutes he was gone, all of the washcloths, tea towels, and linen napkins were incredulously fused to one another, creating a quilt of sorts and it was hung on the only bare wall in the room. He took his phone and created a video of floor, ceiling and walls. On the wall by the door, every knick-knack was turned upside down and backwards, some resting impossibly on the smallest part of each object.

He turned the phone back to the kitchen table, trying to figure out how the creation before him had been made, but in the paranormal, nothing is impossible.

The stacked articles created an archway of sorts. The base item on each side were spatulas standing straight up with the flexible flipper pointing upward. On top of each spatula were Aaron's two small cast iron pans, well-seasoned after nearly one hundred years of use, handed down to each generation. On the outer area of the pans, handles pointed down, resting on the spatulas, spoons, knives, and forks were balanced on the edges of the pans, tines, scoopers and cutting edges pointed upwards. Balancing on them were many, many dinner plates, soup and salad bowls, and three gravy boats. The top of the arch was a hodgepodge of baking pans, canisters, salt and pepper shakers and jars of spices. He stared in wonderment at this assemblage of kitchen items pondering its meaning, when he heard something drop to the floor behind him. The noise startled him so, that he grunted in surprise.

When he turned around, a phone number and a name appeared on the front of the refrigerator, put together with colorful number and letter magnets that were stored in a drawer from when his daughter was a little girl.

He took a picture of the information; 910-555-7334 and CALL RICK CONLEN were stuck to the fridge. No sooner than he took the picture, the magnets crashed to the floor. He looked down and when he looked up again, a new message appeared; YOU ARE NEEDED FOR THE GATHERING.

Aaron once again took a picture and then checked his phone to see if the video and photos were saved. They were. He punched in the numbers.

Wrightsville Beach, North Carolina

1c

As he stood in the center of the bridge, looking where everyone was pointing, talking to Denise, he could hardly believe his eyes. Three large, wooden sailing ships from a time long past were not quite sailing in the water toward the bridge, but rather were moving on a thin layer of air about a foot above the surface of the water. He saw people aboard each vessel, performing the functions that would probably be executed on an everyday basis, had these ships been filled with living crew members.

A man, dressed in a very expensive looking suit, highly polished shoes, pink dress shirt and a black, silk tie, rushed to the railing. "Oh, my God! The first ship is the USS Hunter. It sank in 1861 somewhere off the Outer

Banks and took nearly one hundred men with it to the bottom." He strolled back and stood beside Rick. My great something grandfather perished on that ship. I hope I can recognize him if I see him. His picture has been hung in our house forever." Moments later, he did indeed see him.

The second vessel looked quite a lot like the pictures he had seen of the Nina, Pinta and Santa Maria. Five sails were filled with wind, propelling it forward, yet there was no wind to speak of. The sails were adorned with Spanish markings, so chances are this ship could have been part of a fleet or an armada. Rick leaned toward the latter because he saw cannons protruding from the one side, and he was sure the same would be found on the other side. Again, this ship was filled with ghosts, waving their hands, hats, and pieces of cloth. The sound of laughter was carried toward the bridge on the non-existent wind. He realized it was the Santa Maria when he saw the spirt of Christopher Columbus smile at him. The Santa Maria was Columbus's personal ship.

The third ship was a whaler from the mid nineteenth century. There were crewmen raising a long dead translucent whale from the water. It was the first time Rick had ever seen the spirit of a mammal and he wondered if more of God's creatures would show themselves in their ghostly forms. As he continued to watch the ghosts of sailors retrieve the ghost of the whale, Denise had finally worked her way to the center of the bridge and took his hand.

"Rick, this is really crazy, isn't it? Not only the spirits that are rising, but the number of people that are witnessing this event is amazing."

He nodded. "Crazy isn't the word, Denise." He pointed toward the trio of ships nearing the drawbridge.

I'm rather curious to see what's going to happen when this first ship tries to pass beneath with the drawbridge down. They do look solid, don't they?"

Denise stared at the first ship, less than twenty feet from the bridge, its sails much higher than the closed drawbridge. It did appear solid and she thought she could even hear the sails ruffle, though there was no wind. She hadn't noticed that when she arrived, but the sails were surely filled with air, propelling the ships at a fairly rapid speed.

Moments later, the upper portions of sails passed through the bridge, exiting on the far side.

Rick and Denise reached out and tried to touch rippling sails, wooden masts, small flags, ropes, and their hands passed through everything. Several young kids, not fearful of anything it seemed, raced through the sails, masts, flags and ropes. One of them said, "That tickles, let's do it again" He and his friends crossed through the ghost ship to the other side of the bridge. Unknown to anyone at this time, two days later they would all be dead.

After the three sailing ships passed under and through the bridge, followed by many more ships and smaller craft, the excitement left the crowd. Most everyone headed back to cars, trucks and bicycles. Those who walked or ran went back to doing that, but they would never forget what they had seen today.

Near Bar Harbor, Maine

1a

Samuel and Samantha Staunton, nineteen year old fraternal twins, unzipped the door to their tent and crawled out to last night's campfire area. Sam placed some kindling, that he took from a waterproof bag, on the top of the ash pile after moving some partially burned logs that had been wetted down to keep them from burning while the twins were asleep. He took a match to the raw wood as Samantha shined a flashlight into the fire pit. She looked toward the southeast and saw a faint ribbon of red; the sun was still below the surface of the earth. She smiled because she and her brother would have a beautiful sunrise to witness here in northern Maine.

They were hardly ever separated since they were twelve. Home schooling took the place of public school and their circle of friends would probably be considered very small by today's standards. Neither of them were on any social media sites and one rarely went out without the other one by his or her side. They very seldom saw any relatives, unless there was a marriage or a funeral, and then their appearance would be quite brief.

Their abnormal behavior was precipitated by the death of their parents nearly seven years ago. At that time, both children were normal in every way. They went to school, played with friends, and were often outside, climbing the mountains near their house. Worship was an integral part of their lives since they were toddlers. Sunday school was followed by church services at the local Presbyterian Church and after the service, they often had questions for the pastors, learning as much about God as possible. Samuel entertained thoughts about becoming a pastor himself someday. Samantha, though as devout, was leaning more toward a career in medicine. When she dissected a frog she found lying dead by their pond, she was amazed with all the organs, muscles, and blood vessels she saw.

Those dreams, and more, vanished on July 11th, 2007, seven years ago today. The family had set out for a day trip, leaving the house just before dawn. Steven, the father of the twins, was behind the wheel, while Stella, their mother, rode shotgun. The twins were in the cargo compartment of their brand new Honda Pilot. The rear seats were pulled forward, allowing the kids more room to play and to take a nap if they tired during the three hour drive.

Less than one hour later, a car sped out from a side road. Steven did everything he could to avoid a collision, but to no avail. The car hit the left front end of the SUV, throwing it into a spin. The twins were screaming as their vehicle slid toward the edge of the road. The only thing between them and a one hundred and fifty foot drop straight down was a guardrail.

The Pilot crashed through the guardrail and started heading down the embankment, saved from careening all the way to the bottom by a tree stump.

Several cars stopped and a couple of people rushed toward the accident.

Steven was afraid that the Honda would topple soon and he wanted the kids out of there before anything happened.

A young man was the first to arrive. He surveyed the situation and said, "I don't think that stump is going to hold your vehicle for too long." As he said that, the Pilot lurched forward a couple of inches, precariously close to not having any support at all.

Steven popped the hatch. He yelled to the man, "Hurry, please, and get the kids out and then we'll try to come out the back as well."

Once the kids were out and safe, their parents took off their seat belts and Stella started squeezing her body over the console and toward the back seat. The young man was just behind the back bumper, seeing the SUV begin moving forward and downward a little bit more. He held out his hand, but he just could not quite reach her hand. She stretched toward him and her weight shift caused the vehicle to begin its downward slide.

The children screamed as they saw the Pilot hurtle through space, impacting with the earth and exploding moments later.

Their faith was shattered and neither went to church ever again.

1b

Once the kindling began to burn, he added some dry twigs, and then a couple of split logs to the fire, bringing it up to roaring in no time. Though the air was relatively warm, a morning fire was necessary to brew their coffee. Samantha hooked the four cup coffee pot to the metal rod and placed the rod in the two Y shaped branches stuck into the ground on either side of the fire pit.

As it began to perk, the scent of hazelnut coffee permeating the area, Sam took out his camera and attached a telescopic lens. A thin line of red from the unseen sun bathed the mountain range with color, still offering little light, but beginning to paint the sky with broader streaks of red. The terrain to his immediate front was still dark, but the approaching sunrise brought out the shapes of small shrubs, trees, and a small patch of wildflowers that were just beginning to show their colors. Sam snapped a shot, pleased with the way it was going to look.

When Sam smelled the fully brewed coffee he

yelled out, "Sammy, please bring me a cup as soon as you can. It smells so good."

"You got it, Brother." She looked up to see the sun beginning to crest the craggy tops of the mountains, colored a deep blue. The sky above the sun was still deep blues and blacks, with the undersides of the clouds picking up the redness.

Sam took a few more shots and then he saw two people approaching.

"Sammy, two people are coming this way. I didn't know there was anyone else around,"

She knelt beside him. "Me neither. I wonder who they are and where they're camping. I didn't see any fires last night, did you?"

"No, Sis, I didn't. They're waving. Perhaps they're people we once knew. Guess we'll find out very soon."

The sun rose quickly and light danced in their eyes. It was so bright they had to shield their eyes with their hands. Over the course of the next few minutes, the sun became a burning white light. Sam thought how impossible that was, yet it was happening.

Temporarily blinded, neither of them could see the two people, probably less than twenty yards away.

Sam cupped his hands around his eyes and squinted, but all he could see were two shadowy figures, unrecognizable, even at this short distance. "Who's there?" He asked.

A moment or two later, the sun was blocked by the two people standing in front of them.

The twins were stunned. They couldn't believe their eyes.

Sammy gasped. "Mom? Dad? How?"

Stella said, "Hello, children. We have always been with you, but we weren't allowed to interact in your lives.

You have both grown up to be fine young people, but you need to start living your lives again. Both of you need to find more friends and begin dating."

She reached out toward her daughter, but she was unable to touch her.

Her father pulled his wife's hand back. "We have been earthbound all these years. So close that we felt that we could touch you, and as you think back, you will remember those moments."

Sam said, "How is this all possible. I hope you're not going to say that this is all God's plan or some nonsense like that. We gave up on Him the day you two died and whatever this is, it can't be God that is doing this to us. We both must be hallucinating."

His father said, "No Son. You're not hallucinating. We were sent here today to tell you what God wants you to do." He pointed toward the sky behind them.

The twins turned and were given the privilege of seeing something that no human had ever been allowed to see. Heaven opened up and they saw angels and the face of God. They dropped to their knees and began to pray like they had never prayed before.

Lost in paying homage to God again after such a long time, they had no idea how long they had prayed, but after finishing, relishing their regained faith, they turned around and were disappointed to see their parents were gone.

After they went back to the campsite to pack up and go home, Sam saw a message painted on a rock. CALL RICK CONLEN. 910-555-7334

Sam took his phone from his pocket and punched in the numbers.

San Antonio, Texas

1a

At 3 AM, Kyle Quinlan left the bar, drunk as usual, and tried to find his way home, but this time he was not having any success at all. His apartment was only three blocks from where he stood, but he couldn't seem to find the right direction, aimlessly wandering, ultimately returning to the same spot. It almost seemed as though he was not supposed to leave this particular place. He wondered if had finally cracked, as his ex used to tell him.

1b

After his first tour in Afghanistan, he came home to Julie and he was okay. He knew she had never been thrilled that he wanted to make a career of the army, but because she loved him so much, she acquiesced to his constant demands to be a lifer. He'd say, "Honey, all I have to do is put in twenty years and then I'll be able to retire. There is a pretty good chance that after my service, I'll be able to get a good government job," he chuckled. "Maybe I could even become a mailman and put in ten or fifteen years and collect a full pension. I'd be a classic double dipper." He laughed again.

Near the end of his fourth year in the service, he was sent back again, but this time, all the horrors that a soldier could witness, and be a participant of, in combat, filled much of his tour. Shorthanded, as always, his understrength platoon was sent out way too often, but they were all professional soldiers and knew what they had to do to survive and get home in one piece.

He took his platoon of 34 men out a couple days after he was promoted to staff sergeant. That evening after the pinning ceremony, he called Julie to tell her the wonderful news.

"Honey, that is so great," she said. "The extra money will come in handy and you probably won't have to go out in the field as often. You'll be safer." The last comment sounded more like a question to him.

"Time will tell, Julie. Right now we are still understrength and the rebels have been coming out in the open and fighting more. I think we're getting close to something they don't want us to see. Maybe bin Laden is hiding in one of the caves nearby."

Julie didn't like that comment because wherever he was hiding, he would be well protected and a lot of soldiers could die trying to take him, dead or alive. She didn't want him to worry so she just kept it brewing inside, like most every army wife whose husband was in harm's way.

He picked up on the silence and said. "Don't worry. None of us are stupid and we won't get into something we can't handle. Plus we have artillery and air support to soften up any area we have to go into." He was lying through his teeth, but he needed to reassure her that he was not in too much danger.

"Okay, honey. Call me when you can. Love you."

"Love you too, Julie. I'll probably be out of touch for at least a couple of days, but when we come back in, I'll have time to Skype. I need to see your face again. It seems like forever, even though it's only been about five months."

"Take care of you, Kyle. I am counting the days until you are home again."

She hung up and Kyle let out a great sigh. He had decided that if he got home in one piece, he would resign from the army. He had been studying for the Civil Service exam for several weeks online and it was time to start thinking about getting a real job.

1c

Kyle led the men outside the wire just after dawn. The outposts had reported no movement during the night, a good sign that the Taliban were nowhere nearby, or they were lying low waiting to ambush a patrol. Kyle sent out two men, keeping the point no more than twenty five yards from the rest of the men.

He was sweating profusely as they marched toward the cave filled mountain range. They had been up here before, sweeping the area, tossing grenades into the gaps between rock formations, and then physically checking for bodies, weapons, and documents. The platoon had some successes in the past, but the bastards kept moving around and you just never knew where they could be hiding.

The sun climbed higher in the sky. Choppers started seeking Taliban fighters with miniguns and rockets. Kyle was notified that there was a large force of enemy soldiers hunkered down behind rocks and trees and they'd have to be taken out by his men.

The American soldiers scrambled up the hill, taking fire all the while they were exposed. Three men went down in front of Kyle. Two took bullets to their heads and the third was gut shot. He screamed from the intense pain and Kyle saw him take a pistol from a side pocket. Before Kyle could even utter a sound, the soldier placed the barrel to his temple and pulled the trigger, ending his pain forever.

Kyle scurried into a deep, wide depression seconds before bullets stitched a neat line in the ground just in front of him. Two other soldiers sought shelter in the hole, and the three men ate dirt as more rounds zinged past just above their heads.

When there was a lull from the enemy guns, they fired toward the rocks where they had fleetingly seen a couple of Taliban. After they ceased fire, two grenades came crashing down the hill and over the lip of the depression. Kyle grabbed both of them and covered the lethal devices with his body. Amazingly, neither exploded. The odds of two duds at the same time were probably astronomical, but just before he pulled the grenades under his body, he saw something that he would never forget.

The pitched battle lasted for close to an hour and the men were getting short on ammo. Just as suddenly as it began, the firing ended.

Kyle was certain that what he saw attributed to the end of the shooting, but he would never tell another soul what he had seen. They would have locked him in a rubber room and tossed the key.

Three days later, on another mission, a piece of shrapnel severed his spinal cord and his war was over.

1d

Kyle heard what sounded like cannon fire and he saw flashes in the near distance. He turned his wheelchair around and started moving toward the noise. He looked to his left and right and saw hundreds of soldiers, dressed in uniforms from long ago. They wore white pants, blue and red jackets and high hats. When one of the soldiers reached down to pick something from the ground, Kyle saw a red circle on top of his hat. The soldiers were carrying long rifles, most with bayonets fixed.

They marched past him as though he wasn't even there and when he turned his head to the right, he saw more of them passing right through buildings and vehicles on the street as though the objects didn't exist.

He watched in fascination as they started running, some carrying makeshift ladders. Now Kyle knew he had finally cracked. He was watching Santa Ana's army attacking the Alamo, which he realized was only a couple of blocks straight ahead.

He grabbed both tires, wanting to see a battle that was fought almost two hundred years ago, but his chair would not move. He was thrown off balance and he fell on the street, scraping his face and arms. When he looked up in frustration, wondering how he was going to get back in his chair, he saw the face he had seen all those years ago in Afghanistan. Jesus saved his life then and He offered a hand to Kyle. Kyle reached out and when he touched his Savior, he felt the nerves in his spine and his legs tingle with something like an electric current. Jesus pulled him to his feet and Kyle was healed, once again able to walk.

Jesus smiled at him and then disappeared.

The cannon fire and rifle fire became very intense. Kyle turned and began to run the last couple of blocks to the Alamo. He saw American volunteers firing from inside the structure, while Mexican soldiers started climbing their ladders to get inside.

He watched this for several minutes and then the soldiers he could see, both inside and outside the walls began disappearing until there was nothing left but the silence of an empty street, a couple of hours before sunrise.

Kyle walked to the front door of the Alamo and stared at the graffiti written in what appeared to be blood on the large wooden entrance door. He read the message and immediately called the telephone number written in ten inch high numbers.

San Diego, California

1a

Bernadette Owen loved her job as a security guard on the aircraft carrier Midway museum. She was offered a position on midnight shift, wanting that more than days or middles. She felt more comfortable working at night and sleeping during the day. She didn't go out often because excursions in daylight caused her great physical and mental anguish most times.

1b

Her mother was the town prostitute and her father was one of her unknown Johns. Loretta Owen felt nothing when she was told she was pregnant, and she continued using drugs and alcohol in excessive amounts. One day when she was alone, five months later, she did something she had not done in many years. She knelt down and prayed. She let everything out to God that night, hoping that he would favor her and give her a healthy and happy baby. It was not the child's fault for anything she did and she promised Him she would turn her life around after the baby was born. She would stop using drugs, booze and cigarettes and find a real job. She wanted her child to be proud of her.

The first step she had to take was to move far away from where she was living so she could start her new life without fearing her past would be brought up.

She moved to the suburbs of San Diego without any job prospects, perhaps enough money for six months, if the rent wasn't too high, a trunk and back seat full of personal belongings, and the belief that the Lord would take care of her and her baby.

Loretta was fortunate, finding an apartment that was easily affordable, in a decent neighborhood. Two days after she moved in, she found a job answering phones and typing letters. Her boss's secretary was swamped and the idea of having Loretta help out, even for a few months, would give her enough leverage to get the office back in shape again.

The following week, she left work at lunchtime to meet with her new doctor. Doctor Riegger was an old college friend of her former doctor. He had no problem taking on a new patient and wanted to see her as soon as she was settled. Unfortunately, he was ill the week she moved in.

After the exam, he said, "Loretta, everything looks good. The baby had a strong heartbeat and she is quite active in there. Your weight is a little higher than I would like, but not dangerously so. Just lay off the ice cream for a while and I think you'll be fine."

One day at work, a couple of months later, she started getting labor pains about a month early and she was taken to the hospital by ambulance. Dr. Riegger was already scrubbed by the time she arrived and after a quick exam, determined that the baby was turned and was having difficulty breathing. He was certain the umbilical cord was wrapped around the baby's neck and wanted to get the child out immediately using a cesarean section. Loretta agreed and minutes later she was in the OR.

When Dr. Riegger delivered Bernadette, he turned pale and didn't know what to say. The nurse and anesthesiologist had to look away. Much like a leper, the child's body was covered with discolored patches of skin. Her face was the worst, giving the impression that her skin had been burned off of eighty percent of her head. Even the baby's lips were not immune to whatever the hell it was that Bernadette had.

He handed Bernadette to Loretta and she didn't know what to expect by the look on his face. When she saw her baby, she smiled through her tears. Although Bernadette did not look normal by any means, Loretta was sure that her imperfection was part of God's plan and that someday, she would do something very important.

Loretta took Bernadette home and cared for her, watching her grow by leaps and bounds. When she took her outside, people shied away and the few friends she had limited their visits to a few minutes and after a couple of months, the visits ended.

One day while she was food shopping, she dropped some items from her hands and a man helped her pick them up. They talked a little while, pushing their carts side by side, and he helped her put her bags into her car.

"Would you have time for a cup of coffee or a bite to eat before you have to go home?"

Loretta didn't expect an invitation from him, but she hadn't had a man's company in a long time. Nobody would ever watch Bernadette, so when she went out, she tried not to stay longer than a half an hour. She knew God would protect her baby for the short periods of time she was out of the house. She decided to be honest with him and said, "I have a six month old baby girl at home and she is alone. I don't like to spend too much time away from her."

He nodded and smiled. "It's okay. I understand, but I really would like to spend some time with you."

"Well, if you don't mind coffee and toasted cheese sandwiches, we could go to my apartment and I'll make lunch for you."

"I'd like that, Loretta."

He followed her to her apartment and helped her carry her groceries inside. Fortunately he didn't buy anything that needed refrigeration so he was able to leave his stuff in his car.

She unlocked the door and after they stepped inside, they heard Bernadette cooing. "My daughter is different from other kids and if you are appalled by her, you may certainly leave and there will be no hard feelings."

When she brought Bernadette out, the smile never left Gene Ramsey's face. Bernadette saw him smile and reached out for him.

Loretta handed her baby to him and she hugged him hard. He played with her for the entire time Loretta was busy putting away her groceries and making lunch.

Eight months later they were married.

Gene was what wealthy people would call comfortable at the time her met Loretta and Bernadette. They took Bernadette to numerous doctors and clinics hoping to discover a way to restore her skin, but after years of fruitless search, they realized there was no hope for her. They home schooled her and kept her out of the public eye as much as possible, but, now sixteen,

Bernadette wanted to learn how to drive and go to regular school and meet kids her own age.

She finally got her way and not long after she got her license, they gave their permission for her to take the car and do whatever she wanted to do, but to call them if she had any problems with people making fun of her or being mean in any way.

Bernadette came home less than two hours later, tears streaming down her face. Everyone she saw laughed at her or cringed when they saw her face, arms and legs. A photographer took pictures of her as she raced back to the car and she thought someone took a video of her too.

She realized that she had to go back to being home schooled and when she graduated two years later, she was ready to try the outside world again.

Gene talked often about an uncle who had served aboard the aircraft carrier Midway and Bernadette searched the great ship on the Internet. The more she read, the more fascinated she became with its history. Not too long afterwards, it was announced that Midway would be berthed in San Diego and become a museum. She wrote to the president of the museum and told him how much she would like to be employed on the ship but she would like to work nights because of her skin condition. She enclosed a picture of herself, something she had never done before but several weeks later, she was contacted and asked to come in for an interview.

1d

Now ten years later, she was walking around on the flight deck around 3 AM. The night was calm and stars filled the sky. It was a perfect time of the day for a person to reflect on life and just enjoy God's world.

The quiet was shattered by the sound of an approaching jet. She searched the sky but could not see anything, yet it sounded like it was almost on top of her. Without warning, an F-14 Tomcat landed on the deck with a squeal of tires. She approached it and when she touched it, her hand passed through the fuselage. She quickly pulled her hand out and nearly screamed when she saw the cockpit open and two transparent figures scurry down the ladder.

One said, "You better get ready for a lot of planes, miss. Rick Conlen needs us and you." He pointed to a series of ten numbers painted on the side of the plane. In the distance she could hear the roar of what sounded like many, many planes. She looked up and out, toward the noise and in moments, a large number of aircraft, prop planes, choppers and jets passed over the Midway and then circled back, preparing to land. She knew just about every type of aircraft that had been assigned to the carrier over the years.

She grabbed her iPhone and punched in the number.

Wrightsville Beach, North Carolina

When Rick and Denise left the drawbridge, ships and boats of all sizes were still streaming under and through the drawbridge. They found Denise's car and hopped in just as his phone rang.

He listened for a few moments and then opened her glove compartment, finding a small scratchpad. He jotted down some brief notes because Sam was talking so fast and he didn't want to interrupt him. He wrote down, twins, auto accident/lost both parents, home schooling, no church in seven years-lost faith when folks died. Rick was able to get a few words in when Sam finished talking.

"Sam, all I know is that paranormal activities down here are going through the roof." He told him about the upcoming meeting with Hannah tomorrow and that he hoped she would tell him what they would have to do. "I'll call you as soon as I find out what the game plan is, but I imagine you and your sister will probably have to come to North Carolina sometime in the near future."

He took down both Sam and Sammy's cell numbers and then turned to Denise.

"Honey, I don't know what we have gotten ourselves into, but whatever it is, I'm in for the duration. You?"

"Same, Rick. I think God has a huge job for us and if we don't do it, who will. Of course, now it looks like we're going to have help."

He nodded. Let's go to the Causeway Café. I'm starving."

They got there and found no parking in the lot, having to pull in to the lot in front of Redix and walk to the restaurant.

Just as he stepped up on the porch, his phone rang again. He found an empty table and motioned Denise to get him a cup of coffee.

"Hello, this is Rick Conlen."

"Mr. Conlen, my name is Bernadette Owen and I have something to tell you." She told him about the aircraft landing on the Midway and a little about her life. "I don't know what I'm getting into here, Mr. Conlen, but I'm going to send a couple of pictures to your phone. After you look at them, tell me what you think."

The photos arrived, just as Denise brought coffee. "There's about a half hour wait, Rick. If that's okay with you."

He didn't answer her he was so engrossed in Bernadette's pics. When she touched his hand, he realized she was there. "You need to see these and tell me what you think." He picked up the cup and drank it fast.

She looked at the pictures of Bernadette from childhood to today. She scrolled through the latest ones, seeing the planes and choppers on the deck of the Midway and the pictures of ghostly airmen. Then she scrolled to the final picture-a selfie. Bernadette's face was no longer blemished. She appeared to be healed completely.

When Rick came back from getting another cup of coffee, she handed him the phone. "What does this mean? She sees ghosts and is healed, like you."

"I'm not sure, but if I get a call from someone who was once lame and now can walk...?"

The phone rang again.

Saturday, July 12th, 2014
Wrightsville Beach, North Carolina

1

They sat on the beach awaiting the approaching sunrise.

Neither of them had slept last night, tossing and turning, trying desperately to get some rest, figuring that they'd both be quite busy in the days to come, perhaps weeks-only God could answer that one.

Rick picked up the bottle and poured the remaining few ounces of wine into the glass that Denise held out to him. He laid the dead soldier in the sand and twisted off the top of another bottle of beer, killing the six pack.

After he took a couple of swallows, he replayed the conversation with Kyle Quinlan.

"Hello, this is Rick Conlen."

"Mr. Conlen, my name is Kyle Quinlan and I have quite a story to tell you."

"Mr. Quinlan, I've gotten several calls with pretty much the same opening line as you have. Please, call me Rick."

"Thanks, Rick. I guess I'm a little confused by your response, but apparently I'm not the only one with an incredible story to tell you."

"No, you're not, Kyle. I'll explain later."

"Okay, here goes. I'm an Afghan vet, two tours, divorced, and a drunk, until a short time ago. I don't think I will ever take a drink again, but I've never seemed to be able to keep any promises I've made to myself over the years. Oh, I am a paraplegic as well. I caught a piece of shrapnel that severed my spinal cord and I'll never be able to walk again, or so I thought."

Rick wrote on the scratchpad. Drunk, divorced, paraplegic.

"I closed down the bar a couple of hours ago and started heading home. I only live about three blocks away from where I was drinking, but no matter which way I drove my wheelchair, I kept ending up in the same spot. I sat there, frustrated as hell, wondering why I couldn't find my way home when I heard what sounded like a cannon firing. I looked toward where the sound seemed to be coming from and I saw flashes of light. Being a combat vet, the flashes certainly seemed like explosives detonating. I looked toward my left, and then my right, spun my chair around and looked behind me. Seeing hundreds of men carrying rifles, and then turned toward a cacophony of sounds to my front. The nearly deafening noise sounded like hundreds of muskets and pistols being fired.

"I studied the soldiers' uniforms and realized that in white pants, red and blue jackets, and tall hats with a red circle on the top, I was seeing Mexican soldiers, the uniforms dating back to the time the Alamo fell, 1836.

"I decided to ride to the Alamo, only a couple of blocks away to witness the battle and maybe have some questions answered. I grabbed the wheels and pushed them to move forward, but the chair didn't move. I tumbled out onto the street, seeing more soldiers walking through buildings and vehicles and I even felt a couple of them pass through me as I laid on the street. If they knew I was there, they gave no indication of it.

"With Jesus, in the flesh, helping me, I stood up and headed toward the Alamo. I watched the battle for quite some time seeing the Mexicans climb over the walls and batter down the door, storming inside, killing everyone. The soldiers started vanishing and then I noticed what appeared to be graffiti on the door. It was your name and number, Rick, written in what looked like blood. I picked up my phone and gave you a call."

"Now that everything is over at the Alamo, are you still on your feet?" Rick was curious to see if Kyle's disability was gone forever.

"Hell yes, Rick. I don't think I've ever felt better in my life. What does this all mean?"

"I am a ghost whisperer, Kyle…." Rick talked for quite some time, telling Kyle everything that had happened up to now. "I think God has a mission for us. I am the blind man who can now see. You are the lame man who can now walk. Bernadette is the leper who is healed of her affliction. Sam and Sammy are believers again after their experiences. I will give you a call as soon as I find out what He wants us to do. In the meantime, enjoy yourself and do some of the things you haven't been able to do in a long time. Take care, Kyle."

"You too, Rick. I imagine I'll see you soon."

Rick ended the call and took the last swallow of his beer. He noticed two people walking on the beach, heading his way.

2

The Staunton twins sat down on the sand in front of Rick and Denise, facing them, smiling from ear to ear.

Sam said, "Before you guys say anything, I think you should read this." He handed Rick a single sheet of paper.

Denise cuddled close to him so she could read it too.

Dear Samuel and Samantha,

My name is Hannah and we will meet on Monday in Wilmington, North Carolina. Until then, I have several things I need you to do.

Seeing your parents and speaking with them restored your faith in God. What you didn't understand all those years ago was that He was watching over you, yet you chose to shut Him out and live your lives foolishly. You blamed God for the loss of your parents, and that was the wrong thing to do.

Perhaps you still don't understand why your parents died and you both lived, but when the time comes, you will fathom God's plan for you both.

You must immediately travel to Wrightsville Beach, North Carolina, find a place to stay and meet with Rick Conlen and Denise Scott. They will need your help.

Please enjoy your time at the beach.

Until Monday, when we meet, I will end here.

Hannah

Rick handed the note back to Sam. "How did you manage to find a place to stay? This place is booked solid during the summer."

Samantha answered. "After we found the note on the kitchen table when we arrived at home yesterday morning, my iPad was lying there too. I turned it on, to Google places to stay and when I went to do a search, a page was already open to Carolina Temple Apartments. I called and talked to Steve Wright. He told me the strangest thing had happened. He was sold out and just a few moments before I called a room opened up because the couple that had rented it lost their grandmother and were not able to take vacation. He then said, "I really don't think this is a coincidence, this was planned by God. I'll explain when I see you."

"When we arrived late yesterday afternoon, after finding two open seats on a flight to Wilmington, another rather unusual coincidence because the airline realized it was under booked by two seats. Again, I went online at just the right time."

Sam added, "We know that we're going to do something rather important, but I guess Hannah will tell us what our part will be."

"Well, Hannah told us that we should enjoy ourselves too, so let's make this weekend the best one ever. First thing I think we need to do is take you two Yankees out for some great Southern food. My mouth is watering for shrimp and grits at the Causeway Café."

Once again, the Causeway Café was filled to capacity, and they had to wait for seats.

A coffee pot was set up on porch and a little old man, wearing lavender knickers, long white socks, white shoes, a lime green button down shirt and a red ivy cap was serving coffee

He appeared to be a hundred years old, yet he had such a sparkle in his eyes behind large glasses and he spoke with the clarity of a much younger man.

Rick and Sam went over to get coffee for themselves and the girls and they heard him telling his listeners a story about a woman who was probably a wife.

After he finished his story to gales of laughter, the old man stared at Rick and quietly said, "Are you the ghost whisperer?"

Rick simply nodded and quietly shushed him.

The man said, "Mr. Conlen, I really need to talk to you. It's most urgent."

"Okay, Mr....?" They stated walking off the porch

"Just call me George."

"George. I'm Rick. Pleased to meet you." He put out his hand and George squeezed it with the grip of a much younger man. "So what can I do for you?"

"I've been around for a long time and these ghost visits are troubling me somewhat. I figure God has something on his mind, but why do you think He would want so many people to see all these spirits?"

"Good question, George. I wish I had an answer but quite frankly, I'm pretty much in the dark here, too. Maybe He is trying to tell people that a great many people were not sent to Heaven or Hell after passing on, perhaps because many of the spirits I have been in contact with died violently."

George sat down in a rocking chair on the grass; the other one was broken so Rick stood.

George lit a cigar and then rocked for a while. He abruptly stopped and quickly stood up.

Again, Rick thought he stood up much faster than a man his age normally would. There was something about this man that was familiar but he just couldn't put a finger on it.

"I think they just called your name. Your table must be ready."

Rick looked toward the restaurant and when he turned back to say something to George, he was nowhere in sight, but his cigar was lying on the grass: it was no longer burning. Rick finally remembered where he had seen that face before and he had to laugh out loud, garnering the attention of some people standing nearby. He looked up and said, "Good one, George." He chuckled again as he strolled to the restaurant.

Denise said, "Who was that man you were talking to and where did he go?"

"Honey, do you remember the movie Oh, God?"

"Yeah, I do…" Then she had to laugh. "George Burns. I thought he looked familiar. God does have a sense of humor, doesn't He?"

"He does indeed."

Sam and Samantha shrugged their shoulders.

"George Burns, a long dead actor played God in the movie, "Oh, God"." He waited for that to sink in.

The teenagers nodded and laughed. "God came to us as George Burns. How cool is that."

Breakfast never tasted better.

Just before stepping inside the restaurant, Sam called a friend who knew someone down here that they could rent a boat from. After gobbling a huge mouthful of shrimp and grits and taking a healthy swallow of coffee, he announced. "I hope you all don't mind, but I called a friend, who knows a friend, etcetera, and I was able to procure a small cabin cruiser and a driver to whisk us around wherever anyone wants to go. It is going to be fully stocked with snacks and beverages. There is a chef onboard who will prepare a sumptuous dinner at sea as we watch the sun go down. How does that sound, people?"

"That sounds so awesome, Sam," Denise replied.

Rick and Sammy nodded their heads and smiled.

"Great. After breakfast we'll head back to grab bathing suits and whatever else needed to enjoy the rest of the day. I'll give you guys a call and then pick you up in a cab to head to the Wrightsville Beach Marina."

As the others headed out to Denise's car, Rick went to the register to pay the check. He laid it on the counter.

The cashier picked it up and said, "This check has already been paid in advance and you owe absolutely nothing. The man who paid it even added the tip." She smiled brightly. "He was quite generous, leaving fifteen dollars on a forty-three dollar bill."

"Do you know who paid the check, miss?"

"Not personally. He was wearing those golf pants thingees. I don't remember what they are called...."

"Lavender knickers?"

She nodded. "He said, tell Rick George got it. He also said I should tell you that he'll see you soon on the island."

"Did he say which island?"

"No, sorry. After he paid and strolled outside, a patron who had been standing nearby told me he looked like George Burns. Is George Burns a celebrity or something?"

Rick tossed her a ten dollar bill and replied, "Or something, Miss. Or something,"

5

An hour and a half later, Rick's cell phone rang and he answered. "Hello."

"Hi Rick. Sammy and I are out front in a cab. You guys come on down and we'll head to the marina. I was told we have a rather spectacular yacht at our disposal. They emailed me a couple of pictures. Wait till you see it. It'll knock your socks off."

Ten minutes later, they were standing on the dock, feasting their eyes upon the most beautiful boat any of them had ever seen, and the twins had seen quite a few in their lives, especially before their parents were killed. Rick pointed to the name painted near the bow. They all looked and smiled. The boat was named Heavenly Bliss.

They strolled up the ramp and were assisted on board by a young lady dressed in white shorts, a white t-shirt and white sneakers. She smiled brightly. "Welcome aboard. My name is Missy DeLong and I am here to help you in any way I can to make your day as pleasurable as possible."

Once everyone was on board, Missy took them on a tour of the boat. There were four bedrooms, a kitchen, dining area and a living room complete with a large flat screen TV. The walls and carpeting were done in soft tones of greens and creams. Many of the furnishings were made of wood, mostly teak and mahogany. The boat was as beautiful on the inside as it was on the outside.

"Everything on this boat is at your disposal for your convenience and comfort. The refrigerator is stocked with cheeses, fruits, and vegetables, along with several different beers and wines. There are lunchmeats in case you would like to make a sandwich. There is a whole bunch of different snacks in the pantry. The owner wants you all to feel comfortable. Chef Harvey will be preparing dinner to be served just as the sun is going down and you will dine up on the deck, weather permitting. If you have any questions or needs, you merely have to use your pager to buzz me." She handed them each a pager. "Please have a great time and don't hesitate to page me for anything." She left the foursome to their own, heading back upstairs. She really liked these passengers and looked forward to an easy cruise. Had she known what was going to happen, she would have stayed home today.

As she watched Missy leave, admiring her strong looking legs, Sammy strolled over to the fridge and opened it up. She bent at the waist and looked over the array of foods and drinks, reaching in and pulling out a diet Coke and a plate of assorted cheeses. She came back over to the dining area and sat down. She uncapped the soda and took a healthy pull, set the plastic bottle back down on the table and tore off the plastic wrap covering the cheese. Using a toothpick, she stabbed a chunk of Havarti and a piece of Muenster. She brought the toothpick up toward her mouth and then saw that the others were staring at her. She glared back and said, "What?"

The others just broke into gales of laughter, so she simply pulled the cheese from the toothpick and began to chew, stabbing a couple of more hunks as she ate. She shrugged her shoulders and after she swallowed what she was eating, she said, "Sorry, guys, I'm hungry. What can I say?" She looked at her iPhone and then said, "It's been three hours since we ate breakfast."

Sam shook his head and laughed again. He looked at Rick and Denise. "I swear she has a tapeworm. The woman can eat like this all day long and not gain an ounce. I'd have to run five miles every day if I ate like her."

It was her turn to laugh. She picked up a chunk of hot pepper cheese and tossed it into his open mouth. "He's such an asshole, guys. He does run five miles a day and more. I think now that we've rejoined the human race, he'll probably want to run a half marathon. I know he can do it because I've run ten miles with him a few times and he hardly broke a sweat."

After a few more jokes about one another, the twins settled down.

"It was pretty rough when your folks died, I imagine," Denise asked Sammy although she glanced at Sam, too.

Sam nodded, as she replied. "Yeah, it was. Never in a million years did I think that I-uh-we would lose our parents when we were young. I can still see their faces as the Pilot dropped through space and then when it hit and exploded..." She had to stop and take a deep breath and collect herself, fighting back tears that she didn't want to shed. "Most horrible thing I've ever seen and if I never see another person die, I'll be a very happy woman."

Denise looked at Sam.

"Yeah, it was awful. Plus only being twelve really made the whole thing so tragic. We were just really beginning to appreciate our parents and the multitude of gifts God gave us and then, poof, every dream we had is gone. My dad was the coolest guy on the planet, but I guess I was a normal kid and didn't tell him how much he meant to me and how privileged I felt growing up a rich kid." He stopped, fighting back his emotions and when he relaxed, his face softened. He looked at Rick and asked, "What do you think we will have to do over the next few days, weeks, or God knows how long?"

Rick twisted off the cap of a bottle of beer Denise had put in front of him. He shook his head. "I don't know, Sam. I guess we'll be given our marching orders when we meet Hannah on Monday, but I'm convinced that we're going to be seeing a lot of ghosts because of the gathering she mentioned. I just wonder where countless numbers of spirits can be sent for us to do whatever God wants us to do." Obviously it will be an island, but which one. There are a lot of islands off the coast." He took a swallow of beer as Denise and Sammy placed the cheeses, fruits, veggies and snacks on the table.

"How did you become a ghost whisperer anyway?" Sam asked.

Rick told him and his sister about the accident, seeing Hannah there and the unique gift God gave him; the ability to see spirits through blind eyes. "Last month, I was sitting at a table outside The Pharmacy, a restaurant in Southport, which is about forty-five minutes from Wrightsville Beach. Denise came outside and told me that two customers left without paying the check. She didn't realize I was blind and that I saw the two people, who were ghosts. You see, some ghosts will show themselves to living souls, sometimes in a malevolent manner, which wasn't the case here."

He took a sip of beer and a couple of chunks of cheese. When he finished eating he continued. "A young couple from Wilkes Barre, Pennsylvania, were having drinks inside and they had seen the spirits. The husband, Brian Pederson, came down to visit the battleship North Carolina. His grandfather, Al Pederson had served on board the ship in 1944 and went missing…." He was interrupted by his phone ringing. He answered and listened for a while and then said, "Excuse me, please. I have to take this. I'll be back shortly."

"I'll finish the story for him, if you don't mind," Denise said. "Brian became possessed with Al's spirit and over the course of the next couple of days, we found out that Al was murdered for a few thousand dollars in gold coins and we were able to solve the murder. Since then, he has seen more spirits and miraculously he has regained his sight."

Sammy's mouth dropped open. "This is pretty incredible, isn't it? Rick regains his sight and we regain our faith. I wonder what gifts were bestowed on the other people that will become involved in this mission."

"Did Rick tell you that there were others?"

"No, but I gotta assume that we're going to need more people to handle countless ghosts. I don't even know what God has planned. I just figure that we will need more people than the four of us."

6

Rick returned to the table and sat down hard. He took several moments to look at the three people seated with him and then he smiled. "I've only known Denise for a short time and only met you two a few hours ago, but I now know that the four of us and more people as well will be bonded together for a long time to come."

He stood up and then plugged his phone into a USB port on the television. When he looked and saw the others still sitting at the table, he said, "Come in here guys. I'm going to play the recording of the phone call and then you're going to see a short video that will blow you away. After you view it, you will understand what The Gathering will be all about."

The trio found comfortable seats in front of the sixty inch flat screen TV.

Rick tapped the phone and sat down beside Denise and held her hand.

Audio came from the TV speakers.

"Hello, this is Rick Conlen."

"Good morning, Mr. Conlen. My name is Taylor Halloran. This morning, just as the sun was coming up, I was standing by the 9-11 memorial at ground zero, filming it with my camcorder. I was shooting all the way down to the bottom when I saw what appeared to be apparitions coming up through the base of the memorial and floating upward. I kept filming even though it was scaring the absolute crap out of me. I heard some people scream and diverted my camera toward the sound. A family of four, out early like me, saw the specters and ran from the scene. I turned back to the memorial and when all the ghosts were airborne and gone, hundreds of them, I think, I turned the camera back to the base of the memorial and your name and number appeared in front of my lens, no matter where I turned my camera, the number and your name was the only thing I could see. Then I heard a voice urging me to return home to call you and send you this video, which I did. After I finished, a messenger knocked on my door and handed me an envelope. Inside was a letter from a person named Hannah telling me I had to be in Wilmington, North Carolina on Monday morning at 8 AM. I am to meet you there, on the Riverwalk in front of the Federal Building. Also, when I was at the memorial I had another strange experience. I could have sworn I saw George Burns, but he's been dead for quite some time now. Am I crazy?"

"No, Mr. Halloran, you aren't crazy. Please call me Rick. I'll explain everything when we meet. I'm going to look at the video as soon as we end our call. Do you have anything else you want to tell me right now?"

"No Rick, not at this moment. I have a couple of things I need to do before coming to Wilmington, so unless I think of something else, I'll see you on Monday."

"Okay, Taylor. We look forward to seeing you then. Take care."

"Yeah, you too."

Rick pulled up the video on his phone and pressed play, flooding the TV screen with images of ghosts rising from ground zero. The others leaned forward mesmerized by what they were seeing. After seeing the family run away, the video stopped for several seconds. What came next made them all gasp. They saw Lincoln, Garfield, McKinley and Kennedy being assassinated; every shooter was the one accused for each killing. They saw what happened to the planes and ships in the Bermuda Triangle, wondering if the truth of what happened to them would ever come to light. They saw the planes hitting the towers and the carnage that followed. They were fascinated by the final attack on the Alamo, seeing what really happened to all the men and women defending that old church. Scenes of earthquakes, tornadoes, and hurricanes flashed on the screen. They also saw fiery automobile and plane crashes, ships and boats being sunk.

Rick paused the video and turned toward his new friends. "You have seen so many things, probably at least an hour's worth of images, yet the total elapsed time has only been three minutes and fourteen seconds." He waited until they all caught their breaths. "This final scene is the most amazing piece of film you will ever see in your lives. Are you ready?"

After receiving nods from the trio, Rick started up the video again.

7

After Denise stopped crying and lifted her head from Rick's chest, she looked toward Sam and Sammy. They were both still in some kind of shock and comforting one another, talking quietly. She looked at Rick's face and said, "How...how was this possible for us to see, Rick? I don't understand everything, no, anything at all about what is happening to us and I'm scared."

He stroked her hair and held her close. "I know. Everything we saw seems crazy, but I don't think any of it was faked. How could it be? No one could put that all together in this short a period of time. Somehow we saw all the events as they had happened. The deaths of Kennedy and Crockett really got to me when I first saw the video, but then, at the end..." He stared to sob.

After a few more minutes of consoling each other, they sat down. Sam and Denise wanted to watch again, but Sammy wanted no part of it.

She stood up. "You guys can go through that again if you like, but I can't deal. How all those people could do those things is beyond me. I know the events are well in the past, but that video brought them out and it was just so unreal seeing that all happening. I just don't want to go through it again. I'm going out on the deck for some air."

A few minutes later, Rick had his hand wrapped around the remote control and he was ready to press play when he heard Sammy scream. They all quickly ran up the steps and out on the deck to see what was going on.

An old wooden ship was rising from beneath the water.

The ship appeared to be solid, not like the ships that came down the Causeway yesterday and as it stabbed at the air, it began to come back down until the entire ship was floating in the water. Men were running about on the deck, climbing masts and under the deck, gun ports were opened and cannons were moved into position, filling each port. The warship turned broadside to the yacht and in just minutes the ship was firing, cannon balls bracketing the yacht with near misses.

8

Captain Cyndee Jarous saw the ship pop up from below the surface. She had served for sixteen years in the Navy before she got fed up with the bullshit created by superior officers to climb the ladder of rank, hoping to become a flag officer and really get some major bennies when they retired. The military would have been so much better if the upper crust would not have forgotten that they came up through the ranks and knew what it was like to do the job with pride and not succumb to all the crap levied by the powers that be. If the Navy was run by enlisted men and women, people who did their jobs every day because they liked it, the service would be a much better way to make a living. She knew that nothing would change because there would always be a pecking order and unless you played the game, you'd never even get a chance at bat, because someone who didn't mind jumping on your shoulders to climb the ladder would get there before you and probably knock you back a notch or two for not wanting to leapfrog over a fellow sailor to get ahead.

When the first cannon shots were fired, she immediately went into action, putting the pedal to the medal and steering a zigzag course until the yacht was out of range of the guns.

9

Her dad, Todd, a combat veteran of the Vietnam War, felt the boat leap forward and then from side to side. He took off his headphones and heard the sound of large guns being fired. He raced upstairs to the bridge, nearly knocking down Chef Steven Tolbert who had the same idea.

Todd arrived first. "Cyndee, what the hell is going on?"

As she spun the ship's wheel again, she shouted, "Look out the port side."

He turned and saw the old wooden ship firing its cannons at the forty-five foot yacht. None of the balls were hitting, but he could see the splashes no more than a couple of yards from where he was standing. He saw people scurrying around on deck, lowering a small boat into the water. Moments later a half dozen men were climbing down a rope ladder and boarding the small boat. They were armed with muskets, swords, knives and pistols. One of the men fired his musket and Todd felt the bullet pass by his left ear. He heard that sound too often and he ducked down, losing his balance and falling on the deck, just as his daughter took evasive action by turning hard to starboard.

Todd looked back toward the stairs leading to the bridge and he saw Steve stumble onto the deck when Cyndee turned hard to starboard.

When he regained his footing, he shuffled over to Todd, keeping his head as low as possible. "What's happening, Todd? It looks to me like we are taking fire from a British ship because I managed to catch a peek at the flag."

Just at that moment, a cannon ball landed on the deck between the two men and Cyndee. The fuse was growing short and Todd knew there wasn't much time to react. He sprang to his feet and rushed to the old iron ball, pinching the fuse just before it was ready to disappear into the ball. It would not explode now.

He turned back to Steve. "I have no idea, man. This is not only spooky, but well outside my pay grade." He dared to look toward the old ship and then ducked back down. "I think we're finally going fast enough to put us out of danger, but the men in the small boat are rowing their asses off. I think they want to board us. I'm going down to the locker and grab a couple of weapons."

10

Several minutes before the first shots were fired, David Jarous, Todd's thirty-two year old son, was down in the galley, helping Steve prepare the evening meal for the four passengers. He just finished slicing up carrots, celery, green peppers, onions and lettuce for the salad, putting the fresh greens in a large Tupperware container. He pressed the lid on tight and for a moment swore that he heard the plastic top seal to the bottom. He shook his head, grabbed the container and placed it in the refrigerator. He grabbed a can of Coke Zero and popped the top as he walked back to the butcher block counter. He stopped in mid-stride, once again thinking he heard the sound of the can opening. His imagination was running wild. He hadn't heard any sound at all since he was born, and he was also unable to speak.

He put his soda down on the table, lifted it up and set it down again. He wasn't imagining things; he definitely heard the sound of the can hitting the wood. A moment later he heard screaming from the deck. He raced upstairs to see the woman, Sammy, yelling and pointing toward an old wooden ship that had risen from the water. David saw it level off and moments later, cannons were fired, aimed toward the yacht. He heard them clear as bells and he smiled. Even though the craft he was on was in danger, he was relishing everything his ears were picking up.

The other guests were also watching the ship closely and didn't see Sammy begin to swoon and start to fall.

He rushed over to her and grabbed her arm, turning her toward him. He wondered what would happen, but he had to try. "Are, you alright, Miss?" When he heard his own voice for the first time, he threw his head back and laughed, surprising Sammy, who was fearful for her life and all the other lives on board for a matter of fact.

"Why are you laughing, David? Being fired on by that ship and it sure as hell isn't funny."

"I know, Sammy, but I've been a deaf mute all my life, never been able to hear or speak until just now. But, I think we need to get out of here in a hurry. I'm going to the bridge to see if my sister needs any help getting us out of here."

He hurried to the bridge and when he saw his sister whipping the wheel back and forth, still taking evasive action against the firing, he tapped her on the shoulder. "Can I help you steer this thing, Cyndee?"

Shocked at hearing him speak for the first time ever, she let go of the wheel and wrapped her arms around him for a moment and then as a cannonball chunked against the hull just above the waterline, she took control of the boat again.

Cyndee looked at her brother. "David, how is it possible that you are talking? I don't understand any of what is going on." She pointed. "That ship just came up out of the water and then whomever is on board started shooting at us. It's impossible, you know."

He nodded. "I know. I guess when we get back, Dad'll call the doctor and want me checked out. Hell, I don't know how long I'll be able to hear and speak, but even if it's only for today and I can tell you guys things that I've had in my heart for so long, it'll be worth losing the ability again, if that's how it is supposed to be." He looked around. "Where's Dad?"

She whipped the wheel again. "He went downstairs to get some weapons and he's going to be so surprised."

11

Downstairs, Todd opened the weapons locker. Inside were two .45 caliber pistols, a shotgun, and an M-16 semi-automatic rifle. Many times he was offered the opportunity to make the little black gun automatic and he turned down the offers every time. Now he wished he wouldn't have. He put the two handguns in his belt after checking that they were fully loaded, grabbed the M-16, reliving a flashback to Vietnam for a couple of moments, and then he draped a bandolier of clips over his shoulder. Before heading back up, he heard a cannonball clunk against the side of the boat and he shook his head, totally disbelieving what was transpiring on the ocean. He just could not fathom how a wooden ship, resting on the bottom of the ocean for over two hundred years could rise and bring weapons to bear on a modern craft. Something was bothering him about the cannonball he was able to defuse. When he was able to pull it out from the ball, it seemed too easy and though the fuse appeared to be burning, it was cold to the touch. He also wondered about the men in the boat rowing toward them. The yacht was up to full speed, twenty-five knots and yet the rowboat was keeping pace. That was totally impossible. He was working on a theory and wanted to tell everyone his idea before implementing the use of weapons to retaliate. He hurried to the bridge, wanting to see if the small boat and the ship were still keeping pace.

12

When the others arrived on the deck, they saw David racing away from Sammy, apparently heading toward the bridge.

Sam hustled over to his sister and asked her if she was okay. She nodded and then said, "David spoke to me and he told me it was the first time in his life he ever spoke. How can that be?"

"Todd told me that David has been a deaf mute from birth, but that he is very smart and wanted to help out with the family business. Todd saw nothing wrong with it so David goes out on every cruise, doing whatever else needs to be done besides driving and some maintenance. It certainly seems like him regaining his speech and hearing is about as impossible as my blindness being cured, yet here I am with almost perfect vision. 'Splain that to me, Lucy?" He asked in his best Ricky Ricardo voice.

The others just shook their heads and shrugged their shoulders.

13

When Todd arrived on the bridge, he checked out the position of the old wooden ship and the rowboat approaching the yacht. Even though they were cruising at nearly twenty-five knots, the two old craft were keeping pace; he was right with this theory. Now if his second theory worked, the problem would be solved, but the mystery would still remain.

He saw David's mouth moving, nothing unusual because he did mouth words and sentences often, but Cyndee was smiling so much he thought that she was actually hearing him. He trained his mind back on what he needed to do right now and that was to get the attention of the four guests and motion them up to the bridge. He felt he would need all the help he could get to put his plan in motion.

Todd saw a bullhorn, grabbed it and called out. "Would everyone please come to the bridge immediately." It was not a question, but a command.

He saw them walking toward the ladder and then turned his attention back to his son. "David?" He quietly asked, and was stunned when David turned toward his voice and then his son ran toward him and hugged him.

"Dad, I don't know what happened but after the ship appeared I heard sounds I was making in the kitchen and then I went on deck because I heard Sammy scream. I spoke to her, Dad, and I laughed with joy because hearing my own voice was something I never thought would happen. I don't know how long this will last, but I have so much I want to tell you and Cyndee."

Todd ruffled his son's hair. "I wouldn't worry, David. I think your hearing and speech is here to stay and moreover, I think this was supposed to happen so you can help make that ship, rowboat and men leave us alone."

When he saw the four guests arrive on the bridge he told Cyndee to pull back on the throttle all the way and turn off the key.

She nodded, but with a quizzical look on her face and when the engine was off, she locked the wheel in place and joined her dad, her brother, Chef Steve and their four guests on the port side of the wheelhouse.

"I don't think the ship's cannons, nor the men in the rowboat can cause us any harm, but I think they might have something to tell us. I'm going to use the bullhorn and tell them to board us because I want to know why the ship appeared to us. Does anyone have any ideas?" As he asked this, he looked straight at Rick.

Rick nodded. "It is a ghost ship for sure, and once it is gone, I'll try to explain everything that is going on."

Todd took the bullhorn and called out to the sailors in the small boat. "Come alongside, men and we will allow you to board us. We mean you no harm."

One of the sailors replied. "Leave all your weapons on the bridge and we'll meet on the deck."

14

Once the four sailors, dressed in garb of a long, long time ago stepped on board, the one who ordered for the weapons to be left on the bridge, spoke again.

"Our ship was sunk in 1837. We were carrying spices from Europe to deliver to Virginia when we came under attack by three unknown ships. Night had already set in and the ships came close to us under the cloak of darkness. The four of us were killed when a cannon ball landed near our position on the deck and shrapnel tore through our bodies. Immediately after I died, I realized I could still see everything that happened. Not wanting to risk any more lives, our captain chose to have them board our vessel, which thirty of their men did. They took all of our merchandise, robbed us of all valuables and then shot every man on the ship to death. We want to come to The Gathering and put ourselves at rest."

Rick said, "You and all your shipmates are welcome. Until that time, you need to go back to your ship and return to the bottom of the ocean."

The ancient sailor nodded his head. "That is agreeable to us. We hope to see you all soon, because you will all have much work to do. There are many who will reject the offer of going to their final reward and some humans may suffer and even die at their hands. Prepare well my friends. The mission He has given you is not an easy one, but if your faith is strong, you will prevail."

The spirits on the yacht vanished and when Rick and the others looked out to sea, the small boat and the old wooden ship were gone as well.

Rick turned back to the others. "Todd, David, Cyndee and Steve, I have a lot to tell you and I'm sure you'll want to hear the whole story and see the video that was sent to me earlier. That alone will probably answer a lot of questions, but please ask me anything."

15

Two hours later after Rick told them everything he knew about ghosts, Hannah, George Burns as God, and showing them the video that really blew them away, the ship's crew were mentally exhausted.

Even though their brains were filled with impossibilities, they accepted what they learned, hoping to ascertain much more to prepare for The Gathering.

When he was sure they were ready, David quietly said, "Dad, Cyndee, I need to talk to you both. After learning what we are going to be doing with our lives for a while, there are some things I need to tell you."

Todd and Cyndee had momentarily forgotten about David, concentrating on all of Rick's words and the images on the video. They both smiled at him and nodded, standing up and following him down to the galley.

Father and daughter sat down at the table while David went to the fridge and brought three beers, setting them down on the table and then he took a seat.

David took a sip of ice cold beer, relishing the feeling in his throat as it tickled going down. He had drank many beers since turning twenty-one, and quite a few even before becoming legal, but this one tasted so much better than any of the others. He took another sip.

"I can't believe how good it feels to be able to speak and hear. Reading lips was always a challenge because sometimes you guys would cover your mouths with your hands, but I knew you were still talking. I guess there were things you didn't want me to know what you were saying. The only one who never covered her mouth was mom." He stopped for a moment and wiped a tear. "I really miss her and I hope one or both of you will tell me what happened to her. I don't need to be protected, if that is what you were trying to do all these years." He stopped again, waiting.

Cyndee looked at her father, who had looked downward and began to breathe hard. She knew how difficult it was going to be for him to tell the story again. When he told her, just before she went into the Navy, he was visibly shaken, but she knew he needed to tell her everything. He told her he never wanted David to know because David had enough on his plate to deal with. At that time, her brother was going through a difficult time, being harassed by kids who laughed and made fun of him because of his disability and he was very withdrawn for a long time. When she saw him raise his head, she figured he was ready.

"David, when your mom died, you were going through a very difficult time in life. Maybe you remember or maybe not, but you were always getting slammed by kids in school who were making fun of your inability to speak or hear. Many times they'd even make comments in front of me and your sister and it hurt us so badly to see you being treated like that. We figured it would never stop and every day after you came home from school, you didn't even want to communicate with us."

"Yeah, Dad, I know. It guess it must have taken a year or more to outgrow that BS. I just needed to get comfortable in my own skin and let the taunts roll off me. Even to this day, some of my old friends try that crap on me and then they pick themselves off the floor." He laughed.

"I never knew that, David. I know you really worked hard on your body, making yourself strong, but I didn't know you used your strength in that manner. Glad you took care of yourself, Son."

"I had to, Dad. You were going through so much yourself. Vietnam really took a toll on you and someday I hope you'll tell Cyndee and I about it, but you'll do that in your own time, I guess. I noticed how you and a lot of guys who fought in a war changed when we went into Iraq and Afghanistan, even though I was only a kid. Then after nine-eleven, you even got worse. If it wouldn't have been for Pastor Rob inviting you guys to a meeting and having you all talk freely about your war and the ones going on still, you would have been a basket case."

Todd felt a tug at his heartstrings. He had no idea David knew so much about him and yet there was more he needed to share. He would do that before this day ended. "You're right, Son. I was a mess and it got bad again when Cyndee enlisted but Rob got me through a lot. We chatted often and he really helped me regain my faith. I guess it will come in handy with this mission, won't it?"

David watched Cyndee fight back tears, not knowing her father had that much of a difficult time when she went in the Navy. She reached out and rested a hand on his shoulder and he leaned in toward her.

"Yeah, I guess it will."

There was a long silence, each family member gathering their thoughts.

"I told you that your mother died after getting pneumonia when you were just a baby, but that was a lie, Son. Your mother was murdered one night when I was out at the bar, drinking, trying to drown my troubles away. I really had a bad day at work and when I came home your mom was giving me crap about a couple of bills not having been paid. I ripped into her, screaming and yelling about how hard I was working to keep our heads above water, but the boss was cutting down on our overtime and it was getting tough. You see, kids, I didn't tell her that I was gambling heavily, often losing a couple of hundred a week. Sometimes I was lucky and won big time, but instead of putting that money back in the checking account, I'd eventually gamble it away. I was drinking a couple of cases a beer a week and smoking two packs of cigarettes a day." He took a sip of beer. "You guys know I don't drink too much anymore, but that night, was really bad."

"Dad, if you don't want to go on, it's okay. I really don't need to know." David stood up and went to his father, kneeling on the floor by him.

Todd pursed his lips, closed his eyes and nodded. "No, David you need to know this."

He stood up and they walked up to the deck. Todd leaned over the railing, looking at the water, seeing her face looking back up at him.

He turned away from the image and then faced his son. "I came home and saw your mother lying on the kitchen floor in a pool of blood. Her clothes were torn off and I was pretty sure she had been raped." He began to sob and David held him for a long time before he could continue. "Whoever had done this to her, slit her throat and she bled to death. I was devastated because I should have been home with her and her death had to be my fault."

"Dad, it could have happened to anyone."

Todd looked at his son and shook his head. "No, David. If I would have been home, your mom would still be alive today."

Cyndee had been listening and rushed to her father and brother. "Dad, if you were home, both of you could have died that night. You said you were robbed too, so maybe Mom surprised them and they had to kill her so they wouldn't be caught."

"She's right, Dad. You both could have been killed. I understand why you never told me, but I think I would have understood. Granted, you should not have been drinking, gambling and smoking so much, but many veterans suffered from the same curse you did. PTSD is horrible and you just didn't deal with it at that time. I guess that's why we moved here when I was just still a baby. You didn't want me to read about it or find out from our family and friends."

He nodded and then looked at his children. "Can we talk later? I really need a little time alone."

They squeezed his hands and walked away.

Todd looked into the water again. He didn't know what to do. He felt so bad for the kids, even though they tried to comfort him. He walked around to the back of the boat and then he saw her, standing there, looking just as she did before that night. Tawnee Jarous was a beautiful woman and he fell in love with her almost from the moment they met. She held out her arms and he came.

"Todd, it wasn't your fault that I was killed. True, you were not the best husband in the world when you drank, but even through all that, I loved you till the end. I need you to know that. What happened to me was a horrible accident and it was all my fault. I left the inside door wide open after I brought in the groceries. Apparently a man followed me from town. I shouldn't have dressed so provocatively, but I wanted to surprise you with a nice dinner and a bottle of wine and then hope we could have a talk. I wanted to tell you about a retired doctor I met recently who was also a Vietnam vet. He was on the path to a violent end, but one day it hit him that he had a lot to offer and he needed to straighten out his life. He did and he told me he would be able to help you. Unfortunately, he passed away a couple of years ago. Please don't blame yourself for what happened to me and look after the kids, even though they are grown up and fine adults."

She vanished before he even had an opportunity to respond.

16

For the remainder of the day, the crew quietly did their jobs, all of them thinking about what they had learned so far today and how their lives were going to change; however none of them would ever know how radically.

Todd was on the bridge relieving Cyndee from her boat driving duties so she could take a bathroom break and a little nap. He knew she was really wiped out and she and David still wanted to have a long talk with him. He smiled when he saw several dolphins jumping in and out of the water. He began to wonder if other living creatures had the ability to worry. He realized that they often had difficulties in their world; predators, aging process, lack of food and water, and they probably had concerns about their offspring as well, but was there a worry mechanism built into their minds.

He had a dog when he was a kid and the animal certainly did have emotions. Taylor was often happy, knowing he would always be fed and he would never be thirsty. He would always have a warm, dry place to live. The dog would get plenty of exercise and rewards for doing good things. When he grew older, Taylor tried so hard to please Todd, even to the point where Todd could see pain etched in his eyes: eyes that were quickly dying and his sight would soon be gone. His hips were filled with arthritis and when he tried to lay down, Todd would watch him, filled with sadness that his buddy was growing old. He did view Taylor's afflictions as a precursor to the ailments that might befall him, but at sixty-seven, Todd still felt pretty good. He tried to take a one hour, four mile walk every morning and he was watching his diet, keeping his diabetes in check. He wanted to be around for a long time to come and even secretly hoped that somewhere down the line there might be a grandchild or two.

He heard a noise and realized it was his phone: someone had left him a text message that read-Todd, don't worry about my other living creatures. They will be taken care of and, no, they don't worry, but that was a really good question. Todd laughed and put the phone back in his pocket.

17

An hour later, when Cyndee came back to the bridge, she felt refreshed. She patted her father on the back and said, "Dad, I love you and I want you to know that no matter what happens from here on in, I will never stop loving you."

He nodded and gave her a hug. She watched him walk away with his head held high. She was pretty sure that he would be fine.

As she steered the boat, watching the sun begin to descend, she thought long and hard about her life. At thirty-seven she felt much younger inside. Physically she was in terrific shape. She had run the Boston marathon nine times, and was fortunate to have passed by the location where the backpack was placed two minutes before it exploded. She remembered the fear and the unsettling feeling that a much larger event would happen, throwing the United States into a war frenzy. As she ran back to the bombing site to offer assistance, she thought she had seen two of her fellow servicemen that were killed in Afghanistan, but she shook the vision away and they were gone. After today, she knew that Sara and Matt were there, probably to tell her everything would be okay.

The ocean was extremely calm and the sky was still full of billowy white clouds. Cyndee viewed them all, looking for familiar shapes. She saw one that looked a little like an elephant with one ear up and the trunk tucked against its body. Later she saw one that looked somewhat like an Indian in a headdress. Other than that, the clouds looked like clouds.

A little alarm went off on her iPhone and that was her cue to slowly turn the yacht around and begin heading back toward Wrightsville. The sun, now off her left shoulder was dropping quickly, with probably less than an hour of daylight left. Dinner would be served just about the time the sun set and the lights on the boat would be turned on. She was getting hungry.

18

David was in the galley, helping Steve prepare dinner. They had taken a table out to the deck, covered it with a nice white linen cloth and laid out the place settings for five. His father would eat with the four guests, while he, Steve and Cyndee would dine in the galley. Cyndee would have a limited time to eat, having to return to her driving duties before the yacht drifted too far off course.

Generally she would have a half an hour to forty minutes to eat which would be plenty.

As the two men worked diligently on the fish steak, potatoes, vegetables, soup and salad, David talked like a magpie, making Steve laugh with the stories David always had inside him but had no way to communicate them to anyone. Some things just had to be spoken and now David could talk someone's head off if allowed to do so.

He had just told Steve a joke he heard about three men and a young lady of ill repute. Steve was crying he was laughing so hard and he found it hard to believe that David even knew stories like that. David was sure that Steve still thought of him as a kid, since there was an over forty year difference in their ages.

David just didn't want to stop talking, so he chatted about everything under the sun, well, everything he at least knew something about. If it seemed like Steve didn't like the subject matter or couldn't keep up with him, he'd just jump to something else. One topic that really opened both their eyes was when David asked, "Steve, do you think we are the only intelligent beings in the universe, or are there others out there with whom we could communicate?"

Steve stopped tending to the mahi-mahi that was in a large cast iron pan and he turned down the heat. He looked at David and nodded. "Back in the day, when I was in the Air Force, I was tail gunner on a B-52. We were based on Guam and took a lot of training flights because it seemed as though the shit was going to hit the fan in Vietnam in the near future. This was sixty-three and I was only twenty-one."

He opened the oven door to check on the potatoes baking inside and then he stirred the vegetables cooking in a large wok.

"The food will probably be ready in less than fifteen minutes, so I'm going to wait until cleanup time to tell you the rest of the story." He smiled through the gaps in his teeth.

19

As the four guests watched one of the most incredible sunsets any of them had ever seen, Todd stepped on the deck, dressed splendidly in a white suit, shoes and shirt. In his pocket was a red decorative handkerchief and he wore a red tie. He walked over to the railing and stood a couple of feet to the left and behind his four new friends. They were also dressed to the nines for dinner. Rick and Sam were wearing black suits and highly polished shoes. Denise wore a long dress, lime green in color with dark green high heels. Sammy had on a white mini dress that complimented her long, athletic legs. Her dainty feet were ensconced in red high heels. "Absolutely gorgeous, isn't it? You know, every time I watch the sun rise or set I still find it hard to comprehend that there are so many people out there who don't believe in God." When they turned to him, he saw Rick was wearing a lime green dress shirt and black bow tie. Denise's gown was low cut and afforded everyone a good look at her cleavage. Sammy's mini dress went all the way up to her neck, but she looked ravishing. Sam was sporting a light blue shirt and a white tie. They all looked really good and he was so glad they adhered to his rule of dressing for dinner. There were a few guests in the past that didn't and they were never allowed to book a dinner cruise again.

Rick nodded. "I couldn't have said it better. Even all those years when I was blind, I kept my faith. I am of the opinion that God has a plan for all of us, and whatever we are going to have to do at The Gathering will certainly be a big part of it."

Denise took his hand. "I believe that you and I are going to be together for a very long time and I am also positive that all of us, and those who are yet to come will accomplish some great things in our lives."

Sam and Sammy were quiet, but Todd could see that they were filled with joy and probably also looking forward to what was to come over the next few days or so. He was also looking forward to meeting the other people who came into contact with ghosts and had already seen major changes in their lives, both physically and emotionally.

He pulled out his phone and saw a text from Steve. He and David were ready to serve dinner and asked everyone to please be seated. Todd said, "Please sit down at the table. Dinner will be served momentarily."

Rick pulled the chair out for Denise and Sam followed suite with Sammy. After they were seated, Todd, still standing, lifted his glass, prompting his guests to do the same. "I'd like to toast you all and thank you for a most interesting cruise. Our time on this boat is nearing an end, but, soon…."

He was interrupted by a loud, crashing noise. He turned toward the sound and saw Steve lying on the deck, on his back, clutching his chest. A tray full of plated food was scattered around him and Todd was certain that he was having a heart attack. Out of the corner of his eye, he saw Rick springing into action and in moments, Rick was trying to resuscitate Steve, but after several long minutes, he lifted his head, shaking it. Steve was gone.

Dinner was forgotten about and Cyndee returned to the bridge while Todd called 911 to meet them when they docked. He saw they were passing Masonboro Island, so they would be back at the yacht club in less than a half an hour.

Saturday, July 12th and Sunday, July 13th, 2014
Masonboro Island, North Carolina

1

Darrell and Mandy Fairchild and Jason and Maura Witson, two couples from Steubenville, Ohio, had been exploring the island most of the day, and they were surprised that they seemed to be the only ones camping. Darrell had read about the place and was drawn to it by the satellite view provided by Google Earth. Jason and Maura weren't easily convinced to spend a couple of days away from their electronic devices, especially since both of them owned businesses, with employees. However, Darrell was very good at selling anything and talked them into it after springing for dinner and a couple of drinks, actually, a boatload of drinks. He could afford it, having just sold his latest novel to Random House for a handsome advance. At thirty-three, with seven books carried by large and small booksellers, he and Mandy were comfortable and had no money worries in the near, or far, future. His second book was a thriller titled *Political Affairs.* He still felt it was the best book he ever wrote, even though he sold hundreds of thousands more copies with three other books.

They spent last night a couple of hours away from the beach, because every rental was booked and it was impossible to find a place for one night. They arrived in Wrightsville Beach several hours ago, parked the car in a long term lot and caught the ferry to the island. Loaded down with enough gear and food for a couple of days, they were all ready for an adventure; none of them had any idea that this adventure would cost three of them their lives.

After getting off the ferry, they had to hoof it to the east side of the island to set up their tents. None of them could figure out why they were the only ones setting up camp, but maybe it was early. There were many boats cruising up and down the sound, but none were docking at the island.

Once they started walking across the island, signs appeared at every landing point that the island would be closed to visitors until further notice. Many cellphone calls and emails were sent to the North Carolina Coastal Reserve, but they went unanswered, so all the boats headed back to the mainland. Masonboro Island was deserted save for four people from Ohio

2

Mandy Fairchild, nee Simpson, fell in love with Darrell when she was nineteen. They met in college where she was majoring in philosophy and he was a journalism major, one year ahead of her. She read many of the pieces he had written for the school newspaper and was very interested in meeting this young man with ideas that were "a little out there", as she used to tell her friends. He was a strong believer in UFOs, paranormal visitations, God and angels, and of course, Satan as well. Every article he wrote was filled with quotes from people he had interviewed by phone and online, and his research was beyond reproach; if you didn't believe before you talked to him or read him, you certainly were on the bandwagon afterwards. He had a great many email friends and years later, when Facebook took off, he quickly gained five thousand friends. His Twitter account boasted tens of thousands of followers, and he wrote his fiction with such a passion that his books were just so believable, people demanded more from him. He would not capitulate from his schedule of only writing one book a year, but the pressure from his publishers and fans was beginning to get to him and he needed to get away several times a year and just veg out. She made sure he wasn't bothered by anyone on these mini vacations.

After Mandy graduated, she applied to many schools and hospitals, hoping to begin a career in her field almost immediately. The job market for philosophy majors was at a low point, but she never gave up applying for jobs, finally gaining employment two years later. A large salary was not a prerequisite as she sought employment because she knew they would never want for anything, but she wanted to put her education to use.

She had always loved camping and when he sprang this idea on her, she was all in in a heartbeat. Of course she hoped they would get some alone time, but she really had no problem when he suggested inviting Jason and Maura. They had been friends since childhood but since everyone had lives, getting together often had become a thing of the past. They generally only hooked up a couple of times a year, but were always in contact via Skype and Facebook, even though they only lived ten miles apart.

As she walked across the island, following her husband, who was singing his fool head off, she just shook her head and smiled. They were going to have so much fun, she thought. How wrong she was going to be.

3

Before they stepped on the island, Jason was able to text his staff of five , informing them that he would be out of touch on some godforsaken island his friend, Darrell, found on Google Earth and they would be camping in tents. Jason was not much of a camper, but he and Darrell had been friends for a very long time and he didn't want to let him down again.

When he entered high school, his folks told him that college would not be affordable, but if he wanted, they could send him to a tech school. After he graduated, he wasn't ready for any more school, so he joined the army, enlisting to get computer training. Surprisingly, the military tests showed he had an aptitude for this kind of work, so after Basic Combat Training at Fort Dix, New Jersey, he was sent to Fort Monmouth for AIT as a 25B-Information Specialist. He got out just before 9-11 and learned to write code, becoming proficient in a couple of weeks. He put an ad in the local paper and began to build websites. His business grew and he had to rent an office in town and hire two people to help him out. A couple of years later, he had to get an even bigger office and hire three more people. By the age of twenty-five, he was taking home a six figure income, paying his staff a lot more than the going rate, but he still had to have a hands on role in his business. He hired a young man, Sean Forbes, as one of his first two employees. He had the ability to gain the trust of prospective clients, facilitating a rapid growth rate, as eighty-five percent of those he interviewed hired Jason. Sean was a master at writing code and search engine optimization prompting his promotion to vice-president of the young company less than two years after he started working there.

Jason hated to spend long periods of time away from the company, but Sean very easily filled in for him anytime. Jason rewarded him with a lucrative salary, including four weeks of vacation, plus yearly bonuses. The other members of the team were more than pleased with their salaries as well. Jason had a happy little family.

What no one knew about Jason is that during his tour in Afghanistan, he volunteered to go out on patrol one night because his buddy only had a couple of days left in country and he was going to be a dad; courtesy of a short leave seven months past. That night, the Taliban caught the patrol in an ambush and after a lengthy firefight, three guys bought the farm and seven were wounded. Jason was amazed that he came through it without a scratch and the combat never bothered him mentally until he was home for about a year. At that time, he was shopping for groceries and a young Muslim man accidently bumped into him in an aisle. Jason turned and saw the turban and his rage just got the best of him. He waited until the man got to his car and then he beat him senseless. Fortunately the man lived and Jason put a couple of thousand dollars in an envelope and slipped it under the man's door. He was trying to make good by his anonymous donation, but he knew he would have to be careful to never let anything like that happen again.

He looked over at Maura and smiled. She was the only person he ever told about what he did and she was never afraid of him. How that would all change in less than seventy-two hours.

4

Maura was one of those silver spoon in the mouth kind of kids, but as she grew up, she drifted away from her parents, and the golden goose stopped laying eggs. She knew that the Internet was going to be the place to make more money so at eighteen, fresh out of high school, she took off for New York City to learn what she always had a hankering to do-Travel and Leisure.

After graduating, she pounded the pavements of the city, applying at every travel agency she could find, and finally, on her seventeenth attempt, she was hired in an entry level position. She worked hard and learned the ropes of giving the customers amazing deals and one day, two agents called in sick. She was asked to fill in and just had one of those days she could have only dreamed about. She booked nine major trips and three weekenders. Damn near impossible, yet she did it. That day cemented her into a position as a full time agent with a raise, bonuses, and the knowledge that she could someday open her own agency.

Two years later after winning countless sales awards, and making a ton of money to boot, she left her lucrative position and headed back to Ohio to open her own agency. She met Jason that year and they started dating, marrying sixteen months later. Bernice and Bernard, their twins, came along later and life was so good.

She imagined being psychic may have led to many of her successes, and if only she had known what was going to happen on this island, none of them would ever have come here.

5

Jason and Maura reached the east side of the island first and when they looked out over the expanse of the Atlantic Ocean, they were both so glad they came.

They set up their tent and Maura grabbed some of the wood they transported to the island to build a campfire. She had just got the fire lit when Darrell and Mandy arrived, tossing their stuff on the sand. She looked up and smiled. "Found a place for a quickie, did we?" She laughed.

Darrell turned three shades of red, but Mandy just nodded, beaming from ear to ear. "Didn't know how much alone time we would get with you two here, so we took advantage of the ten minute gap we created. What sucks is having all this sand in my crouch. I think I'm gonna get into the water as soon as I can."

Darrell shook his head and laughed. "You never were one to keep anything from anyone, were you, honey?"

"Not a chance, dude. If there is something to say about a good thing, I'm the person to shout it to the world." She cupped her chin with her clenched hand, as though deep in thought. "Might be a great post for Facebook when we get back." She looked at her husband. "Shame I didn't take a couple of pics of us doing the nasty. Wow that would have heated up some PCs for sure."

Darrell got red again and smacked her on the behind. "You, young lady, are going to have a stern talking to a little later."

She cupped her hands around her mouth and pretended to whisper to Maura. "Maybe, if I'm really a bad girl, he'll spank me."

The couples were in animated conversation as Darrell and Mandy set up their tent. Maura added more wood to the fire, and once all the work was finished, Darrell walked down to the beach and waved at someone or something that the others didn't see.

Soon, a couple of jet skis pulled up to the shore and Darrell motioned for Jason to come to the beach. They unloaded a couple of coolers filled with ice, beer, wine, cold cuts and cheeses. They also brought a good supply of lumber to burn.

Darrell took out his wallet and handed each of delivery guys a hundred dollar bill and set up a return visit for Monday afternoon. They might be roughing it, but roughing it wasn't going to be too bad now.

After drinking a couple of beers and eating some salami, pepperoni, ham, turkey, and roast beef along with some hot pepper, Muenster, Havarti and horseradish cheddar chunks, the foursome changed into their bathing suits and headed out to the Atlantic. The water was very warm and the waves were softly breaking, making their swim time quite refreshing.

They splashed in the water for less than an hour, not going out too far because rip tides were always possible, and the swimming was just enough exercise to relax them.

Jason was the first one out, racing to the campsite, opening a cooler and popping the top of a Sam Adams Summer Lager. It tasted so good and he enjoyed every drop as it slid down his parched throat. He toweled off and then sat down on the sand, watching his three friends fooling around in the water close to the beach. He stared at his wife. She was so beautiful, and her figure was fantastic even after having twins. She worked out at the gym with him at every opportunity and tried to get a three mile run in every morning. He did not have her determination to keep himself fit, and sometimes he lapsed, gaining a couple of pounds, generally around his waistline and then he'd have to bust it twice as hard to get back into shape. Maybe he'd get better with his daily routine in the near future.

Mandy and Maura hustled to the tents, also going right for the adult beverages. The beer would probably be the first thing to go, as all of them liked a little wine in the evening. Hopefully there would be some cheese left over as well.

Once they had beers in hand, they sat on the sand next to Jason. Maura poked his belly and said, "Gonna have to put you on a diet when we get home, Mister. I sure don't want a flabby husband hanging around the house like a sloth, wearing wife beaters and boxers, farting and scratching his nuts because he hasn't bathed in three or four days. Nor a husband who's face hasn't felt a razor in a long time. No, sir, no one like that for this woman."

Darrell had arrived and grabbed a beer just before Maura went into her tirade. He just shook his head and roared, joining the laughter of the both women and even Jason.

Jason jumped on his wife and said in his best pirate voice, "Har, woman, me thinks you would love to see a caveman type, so's he could rip off your clothes and have wanton sex with you. Har." He tickled her into submission. "Do you want a caveman, woman?" He kept tickling her.

"Yes, yes, anything for you. Just stop tickling me."

He stopped and said, "You're right, I have packed on a little weight in the last few weeks. Too many lunches and dinners with clients and not enough time in the gym. When we get home, I promise I'll get rid of my love handles and you'll love me even more than you do now." He covered her with his body and kissed her passionately.

Mandy threw sand at them and yelled out, "Get a room."

They bantered for a good long time, just basic bullshit, and then decided to take a little nap. When they awakened, just before dusk, they were treated to the sight of a yacht and what appeared to be a small dinner party on the deck.

Maura felt that something was going to happen on that boat and then she 'saw' someone carrying a tray and then falling forward, crashing onto the deck. She was sure the man had had a heart attack and she didn't think he was going to survive. The boat was not too far away, but she didn't think she'd be able to yell loud enough for the people to hear her. Music drifted toward the beach and Maura figured it was just loud enough for the people not to hear her.

She continued to stare at the boat and about ten minutes later, she really saw a man fall forward. The boat's engine was soon roaring as it started gaining speed, heading past Masonboro Island, probably heading to the nearest dock to get the man some help. She closed her eyes and 'saw' that he had died.

After a restless sleep, Jason awakened. During the night he heard sounds, like the whispers of a room full of people talking softly in small groups of twos, threes, and fours, but hundreds of people doing it at the same time. Three times he was awakened by these sounds, and although it was unsettling, he didn't want to disturb Maura by opening the zipper to the tent and checking around outside. The quiet noise didn't last long, but happening three times seemed a bit much. He looked at his watch, seeing that the last time he heard the noise was only an hour ago, which would have made it just before sunrise.

He sat up and rubbed his eyes and then took a couple of deep breaths. He then heard what sounded like metal touching metal and he could have sworn he smelled bitter coffee brewing. Not possible, Jason thought: nobody is on this island, at least not that we know of. He listened some more and then he was certain he heard voices.

Jason, slid out of his sleeping bag and slowly worked his way around Maura and unzipped the door. He looked out and stifled a scream. Just outside the tent, he saw a handful of soldiers, two in blue and three in gray. They were sitting on logs around a campfire, drinking coffee and eating what was probably hardtack. One of them, a Reb, looked toward Jason and nodded. One of his eyes was gone and his uniform jacket was covered in what could have been blood. "Mornin' Yank. Hope you slept well." He said, with what sounded like a mouth full of pebbles.

Jason was frightened, yet he was curious, so he crawled out from the tent and stood up. He did a complete three hundred and sixty degree turn, seeing figures all over the island, as far as he could see. "Maura,

Darrell, Mandy," he called, loudly. "Get out here quick. You're not gonna believe what you'll see."

They heard Jason and quickly got up. When they exited their tents and stood up, looks of disbelief and loud gasps were etched on their faces and uttered through mouths open wide. Their eyes tried to take in all they were seeing.

Maura knew she was looking at spirits from all time periods according to the clothes they were wearing. The ghosts seemed to just be hanging out, not causing any trouble and not trying to frighten the four humans in their midst, but she had no idea why there would be so many spirits together in one space. She wasn't scared because she felt something remarkable was going to happen in the not too distant future.

Darrell was taken aback by the sight of at least several hundred ghosts, rooted to the earth, hardly moving from where they stood, staring at him and his three friends. This experience would make a hell of a novel, he thought. He walked toward a group of men, clothed in buckskins, carrying Kentucky long rifles. As Darrell grew closer, one of the men came toward him, cradling his rifle in the crook of both arms. "My name is Crockett and I don't know where we are, nor why we were brought here. I know this is neither heaven nor hell, but somewhere on earth, since we have been bound here since thirty-six. Who are you four humans and why are all these spirts gathered here?" Davy Crockett saw the look of surprise on the man's face.

After recomposing himself, amazed that he was being addressed by the legendary Indian fighter, he replied. "My name is Darrell Fairchild. We are on a barrier island, named Masonboro, which is just off the North Carolina coast. My wife, my friends and I are here for the weekend camping, and honestly, that's about all I can tell you. I don't understand what is going on, but I have a feeling that all of us will know in the not too distant future."

Davey placed the butt of his rifle on the ground in front of him and leaned on it with his left hand while he extended his right one toward Darrell.

Even though he didn't think he would be able to shake hands with the Colonel, he put his hand out and was flabbergasted when he felt his flesh touch the flesh of a man dead over one hundred and seventy-eight years. Crockett had a firm grip and they shook hands for a long moment before Darrell let go first.

"Mr. Crockett, I don't know for the life of me how I could shake hands with a spirit, but now it truly makes me believe that something, only God could cause to happen, will take place soon."

9

Mandy and Maura walked among the spirits, seeing both smiles and frowns. The scowling spirits seemed to radiate hate and both women were able to detect differences in friendly versus frightful spirits. One difference was the quite distinguishable curvature of the mouths, and as they walked amid the spirits, that difference was very noticeable. The eyes of the hateful ghosts were darker in color than their counterparts. The hateful appearing entities, were gravitating toward their own kind while the others shied away from them, so boundaries were forming, making it easier for the women to figure out who went with whom.

Maura approached one spirit, a young woman. She wore a long black dress, black gloves and a black hat with a very large circular brim. She hid behind a parasol but closed it after Maura said, "Don't be afraid, Miss, I'm not here to cause you any harm. I'm probably as much in the dark as you are, or more, and maybe we can both get to the bottom of us being here on this island." Maura stared at her face. The young lady was gorgeous, although her skin color was extremely pallid. Her paleness was enhanced by ruby red lips and coal black eyes, set beneath even blacker eyebrows. Maura was entranced by her beauty.

The woman nodded. "I am Sylvia Applegate and when I died I was only twenty-two years old. I was out for the evening, hoping to have dinner with a man I had only met two days before. We shared a carriage ride in Philadelphia, discussing the luncheon we had both attended. My father was a very wealthy man and we were attending the luncheon to donate fifty thousand dollars to the Philadelphia Museum of Art. My father was a huge collector of art and he had also planned to give a number of paintings and sculptures to the museum after he passed on. The gentleman I met, Oliver Georges, was a philanthropist as well. His family owned seven factories that produced fine furniture, tapestries, sewing machines and shoes. Oliver was also at the luncheon to donate twenty thousand dollars to the museum. He had a large collection of art, many pieces already on loan to museums around the country. I stood outside the restaurant that night when two men approached me and told me that Oliver had been in an accident and was resting comfortably in the hospital. Of course, I believed them and when they offered to take me to him, I did not hesitate. I got in their carriage and was immediately bound and gagged. They told me nothing would happen to me if my father paid them one hundred thousand dollars for my safe return. Several days later, after having been locked in a room, given very little to eat, and, unfortunately, raped a number of times, I was told that my father refused to pay. They took me to the river, cut my throat and dropped me in. My body was found the next day."

Maura gasped when Sylvia raised her head, exposing the ghastly knife wound from the base of one ear to the other.

"I hated my father from the moment my kidnappers told me he wouldn't pay and I used my ghostly powers to frighten him to death and I imagine that is why I have been earthbound for all these years. I don't believe I will be seeing the gates of Heaven any time soon, and I dread what awaits me in Hell, but I hope this gathering means that all of us locked in the spirit world will finally be sent to our final reward or…," She stopped talking and turned away from Maura.

10

Mandy found herself drawn to an elderly man in a wheelchair. As she neared him, she felt the hair on the back of her neck stand up, but the fear that was building was overshadowed by the need to see who was in that chair and why her nerves were tingling through the roof. Her hands trembled and she could feel perspiration being released from every pore in her body. She looked at her arms and they were glazed with sweat. Her shirt began to stick to her breasts and the uncomfortable wetness seeped through her shorts and made sand cling to her bare feet. Tears ran down her cheeks by the time she saw the man's profile and she cried out when she saw his face.

"Grandfather. Why are you here? You aren't dead? I saw you only two days ago and you were fine."

Her grandfather looked at her through eyes that had seen too much in his ninety-one years. Eyes that were now seeing the people on the other side. He had seen spirits when he was alive: twenty- seven men that he killed, each with only one shot from his sniper's rifle back in 1951 and 1952. Gooks, all, but still human beings doing the jobs they were called to do for their country, just as he was trained to do his.

Leonard Simpson took his granddaughter's hand in his and closed his eyes for a moment; it did no good, the faces were still there. "Mandy, I couldn't take it anymore. All these years I carried the memories of what I did in that war and I couldn't live one more day. After Mother made sure I was seated comfortably in my chair before she went out for her morning walk, I took my pistol from the nightstand, wheeled myself out to the front porch to see the mountain one more time. I placed the barrel inside my mouth and pulled the trigger. Moments after I died, I felt myself being pulled from my body and I stood on the porch, seeing Mother walking down the pavement. She must have heard the shot, even though I thought it would be muffled and when she stepped up on the porch, she wailed. I never heard her cry like that in her life, even after we lost your brother, our only son. I regretted what I had done and even though I was dead, I prayed to God for forgiveness and to look after her. She will enjoy good health until she dies at the age of a hundred and seven. There are many things we learn after we pass on."

Mandy knelt by his chair, not understanding why he felt he couldn't go on. He'd been dealing with his personal ghosts for over sixty years and now he was gone, yet he was still here, on this mysterious island, talking to her. She kissed his cheek. "I am so sorry you had to kill yourself, Grandfather. Mom-Mom must be devastated. Darrell and I will go to see her after we do whatever it is we have to do. Can you tell me what we are supposed to do here?"

He nodded. Sometime tomorrow you will be joined by several people and with their strength and help, you will participate in sending earthbound spirits to their final reward. I can't tell you any more than that, but, know this, child. You will survive and after this is over, you will be stronger." He smiled and looked up toward a light that was reaching downward. "God wants me, now. Sweetheart. Be strong and many wonderful things will happen in your life, a life that will be long and filled with many good things."

Just before the light swallowed him, Leonard Simpson stood up, free of the chair he was a prisoner to for over fifty years. She watched him rise until she could see him no more. Then she stood and headed back to the beach. She had a lot to tell her friends.

Sunday, July 13th, 2014
Wrightsville Beach, North Carolina

1

Rick and Denise had just finished a long, exhilarating run, but before they were able to return to their room for much needed showers, the desk clerk called them over to the check-in counter.

"A package was delivered for you both last night, just after I came on duty, but I was given strict instructions not to release it until this morning. The amazing thing is that I was told by the delivery person that I would see you at this very time. Odd isn't it?" He handed the package to Rick and when they were in their room, he placed it on the bed and opened the envelope taped to the top of the box.

Rick and Denise,

Inside this box you will find everything you will need to complete your mission. Bring   the contents with you tomorrow because they may be needed while you are on the battleship

North Carolina. Your team actually arrived here yesterday and you will be meeting with them tonight at the South Beach Grill. Your waitress will be Sherrl Wilhide. She will be easy to   find because she has spiky multi-colored hair. You two will arrive before the others so you will have a little time to study your soon-to-be new friends.

After you accomplish your mission on the battleship, I will tell you where you will be   going for The Gathering. There, you will meet the remainder of your team.

Until tomorrow,

Hannah

After Rick read the letter aloud, Denise opened the box and they both had to laugh. Inside were twelve plastic squirt guns, a dozen pairs of non-prescription glasses and twelve 8 ounce bottles of water.

"We're going to send the earthbound spirits away with these?" Rick picked up a squirt gun and pointed it at Denise, pretending to shoot her. She fell down on the bed, clutching her chest, but then she abruptly sat up. "This really isn't a laughing matter, Rick. God wants us to do this for Him and even if it's just squirt guns, glasses and water to use as our tools, this is what we must do."

"You're right, honey. Look at what God has given us already. I am so blessed to have you and to have my sight back. I can't wait to meet everyone later." He stripped out of his shorts and t-shirt. "Last one in the shower buys lunch." He started backpedaling toward the bathroom, but he tripped over one of Denise's shoes and fell down.

Taking advantage of his minor incapacitation, she stripped as she ran, just beating him inside the shower by a few moments. She turned on the water, but when she felt how cold it was she jumped out and bumped into him. They looked each other up and down and the shower was forgotten about for fifteen minutes.

2

In another room in the hotel, Kyle Quinlan pulled back the drapes covering the patio door. He opened it and stepped outside, cup of coffee in hand and then he sat down on a comfortably padded deck chair and turned on his iPad. The sun had been up for over an hour, providing warmth that washed over him. He had been feeling quite chilly since seeing the battle of the Alamo unfold before his eyes, witnessing the type of slaughter he experienced in Afghanistan, but on a much larger scale. The most difficult thing to watch was the hand-to-hand combat with bayonets. Each time a soldier from either side was killed in that manner, the soldier who did the killing had the most ludicrous look of horror etched on his face. Killing another human being at long range with pistols or rifles, or in current times, bombs and shells launched from great distances from the battle proper, did not give the soldier the type of anxiety found in close combat. Not that there was insensitivity to taking another person's life, but everyone who had to do it, knew it was kill or be killed, and you'd deal with the physical and mental anguish later.

He picked up his iPad and scrolled the Lumina News finding the community section. He read a story about five teenagers who had just died two hours ago. Apparently they had all become ill Friday morning, after coming home from the Causeway drawbridge where they each told their parents about the ghost ship sails they ran through. Even though all the boys told the same story, no one believed them. The reporter had also interviewed some people who had called telling him about the ships passing right through the closed drawbridge as though the steel and concrete were not there at all.

Kyle took a sip of coffee and then continued reading. The boys were admitted to the hospital on Friday night, screaming and kicking, clutching their throats and their abdomens. All of them were also seen squeezing their heads to the point that doctors and nurses had difficulty pulling their hands from their heads. Although given massive amounts of antibiotics because all the boys had wounds on their hands that were bleeding profusely, painkillers, and sedatives, their wailing never ended until about an hour before dawn. Incredibly, the boys all died at exactly the same moment. Moments after they died, hospital personnel from each of the boys' rooms witnessed what appeared to be apparitions hovering over the bodies.

With his hands shaking uncontrollably, he had to set the iPad on the table. He fumbled in his robe for his pack of cigarettes and lit one up. Smoking was actually prohibited on hotel grounds, but at this point he didn't give a crap. His nerves were getting the best of him and he needed the nicotine to settle him down. Somehow, smokers always believed that nicotine settled them down, but it really did quite the opposite, making the heart race and depriving the smoker of oxygen.

After he ground out his cigarette on a saucer, and grabbed another cup of coffee, he continued reading the article. He finally realized that only a small number of people would know about the thousands of ghosts that were migrating south. The Gathering would take place somewhere nearby at a still undetermined time. In the story about the kids, the reporter stated that he shrugged off the possibility of a supernatural event but he still wrote the story as it was told to him. Kyle figured a story like that would certainly be published on the online issue, but the publisher would probably have reservations about wasting ink and paper to serve it to folks in the print issue. He clicked a link to his local paper and scanned Friday's, Saturday's and Sunday's issues and not one word was offered about what he saw; of course, he was probably the only person who saw the battle.

3

Three floors above Kyle's room, Bernadette Owen kept looking at herself in the bathroom mirror. She still couldn't believe how beautiful she really was, after a lifetime of disfigurement. She touched her face often, marveling at how wonderfully soft her skin felt. She disliked touching her face in the past, but now, she had no problem feeling her skin. After several minutes of looking at herself, she strolled back into the bedroom, ogling her body. Miraculously, after placing her hand on the fuselage of the airplane piloted by ghosts, she felt a tingle pass through her body and the pounds just dropped from her frame until she was the perfect weight for her height. She was certain no one would recognize her and found that to be true when she went home to pack. She told her mom and dad what had just happened, but they didn't believe her, although they could not dismiss the factual evidence her face and body presented to them.

When that plane disappeared, another landed, and disappeared shortly after it touched down. Two hundred and thirty seven aircraft, including helicopters, landed and disappeared shortly thereafter. She recognized most of the different types of planes, even the ones that had flown back from wherever they were suspended after being shot down or whatever means ended their service and took the lives of those aboard. There were aircraft from World War Two, Korea, Vietnam plus different aircraft built after those dire times in our history.

She didn't know what the near future held in store for her, but she felt, with every fiber of her body, that she would live a long life. She hoped she would meet a wonderful man, marry, have children and grandchildren and die at a ripe old age. She felt it was owed to her and then she remembered a sermon she heard a couple of weeks ago. The theme was hymns and the hymn Pastor Cody spoke about was "Jesus Paid It All." He quoted the remainder of that first line saying, "All to him we owe." He reminded the congregation that God owes us nothing, but that we owe all we have to Him. She would have to remember that and live her life accordingly. If God would want her to have a husband, children, and grandchildren, along with a long life, she would have it. If not, she would accept whatever life dealt her, prayerfully hoping that everyone could feel this way. As she dressed, she hummed the tune and just kept feeling better with every passing minute.

At eight-thirty in the morning, Aaron Pammer pulled into the parking lot of the Causeway Café. He wanted to leave Hellertown on Friday, but his Subaru Forrester wouldn't start. After getting a jump from a neighbor, he took the car to a nearby service station. The attendant told him that not only would he need a new battery, but his catalytic converter needed to be replaced. With only seventy two thousand miles on a vehicle that was in terrific shape, he accepted the necessary repairs. The garage owner's daughter called him the next morning around eight to tell him the Subaru was ready. He walked to the garage and then drove back home to pack for his trip to Wrightsville Beach. Aaron felt a little tired and took a nap, not getting on the road until around 3 PM. He stopped for the night, leaving a three hour drive for the next morning. Now he was hungry as a bear. Three years ago, a friend told him about the restaurant and said that if he ever went to Wrightsville, not to miss breakfast at Causeway Café.

He strolled up on the porch and then stepped through the front door. The place was packed and by the look of the number of people on the porch, he figured it would be quite a while before he would be seated. He was actually surprised when he was told that there would be a single available in less than fifteen minutes. He was okay with that.

He walked back out on the porch and smelled coffee. He looked to his right, seeing a little old man wearing thick glasses, a red shirt, red and white diamond patterned knickers, red stockings, white shoes and a white baseball cap sporting the St. Louis Cardinals logo, serving. The smiling man was serving coffee. He stepped over to the counter.

"Good morning, young man," he said, as he poured Aaron a cup of steaming coffee. "How are you today?"

"Fine, thanks. And you, sir?"

"Better than yesterday, but not as good as tomorrow."

When Aaron offered a quizzical look, he added. "I'm an optimist, so the next day should be better than the one before. I just like to keep a positive attitude in a not so positive world."

Aaron lifted his cup in salute. "I'll certainly drink to that, my friend."

"Please, call me George."

"And you may call me Aaron." He noticed an empty stool and took a seat.

"So, where do you hail from, Aaron," George asked, pulling up a stool beside him.

"Born, raised, and lived all my sixty years in Hellertown, Pennsylvania."

"Nice country up there. Been there a bunch of times in my lifetime. I won't give away my age, but it would be safe to say that my face and body don't really show my years."

Aaron looked over his coffee cup and studied George's face. The man appeared to be at least ninety, so how much older could he be. Perhaps he'd find out before he was called for breakfast. He thought about an older gentleman he once knew. His father had passed when he was only seventy, leaving his mom alone. She never wanted to date, but after meeting Vinnie who also was working as a volunteer at the local hospital, they began seeing each other. Mom passed away two years ago at ninety-five, and Vinnie was still going strong. He would be ninety-eight next month. He 'came back to earth' after seeing a large number of people heading inside. He took a sip of coffee and looked at George.

George smiled. "You don't recognize me, do you?"

"No, should I?"

"It'll come to you eventually, son."

George's voice, though a tad gruff, was soothing and Aaron began to feel he was in the presence of a great man, but he still couldn't put his finger on it.

They chatted for a few more minutes and then the hostess called his name. Aaron stood up. "Nice meeting you, George. Perhaps we'll meet again sometime."

"Oh, we shall, Aaron. Rick will tell you who I am. See you soon."

Aaron stood there mesmerized, dropping his cup to the floor as he watched George fade out to nothing. He then realized whom he had been conversing with and he smiled, ready to take on the challenge he was sent here to participate in.

Later, after he checked in to the hotel, he grabbed his camera and went outside to begin shooting what would become the most sought after photo journal ever published.

5

The tall buildings were being colored with God's paintbrush and he always found those moments spectacularly inviting to his artistic eye. No painter or photographer could quite capture the natural beauty of a sunrise, although the paintings and still pictures were quite breathtaking when viewed by the human eyes.

Taylor Halloran watched the skyline of New York City fall further and further behind until there was nothing left in his rearview and side mirrors. He figured he had about an eleven hour trip ahead of him, so he had left just as dawn was breaking to the east.

He had stopped for lunch and was back on the road by 2 PM, figuring he had about three hours more to drive. Though he was tiring, a hot cup of coffee was in the cup holder on the console and Hank Junior was playing on Sirius radio station Willie's Roadhouse. He was singing about his family tradition, one of Taylor's favorite songs.

Taylor sang along and after the song ended he reached for his coffee cup, not realizing that he had also turned the steering wheel just enough to throw his 2003 Honda Civic into the path of a tractor trailer barreling down the road in excess of ninety miles per hour. Taylor just caught a visual of the huge Mack bearing down on him from the corner of his eye, but it was too late for him to avoid being hit.

Three hours later, his body was removed from what was left of the cockpit of the car, buried under the cab of the rig.

Now instead of participating in ending the existence of earthbound spirits, he would be one sent to Heaven or Hell in the very near future.

Sunday, July 13th, 2014
Southport, North Carolina

1

After receiving a call from a client, Rick decided he had to return to Southport for a couple of hours to talk to her. Denise enjoyed assisting him in his law practice and didn't hesitate for one moment to come back with him. She was certainly interested in how he would deal with a client now that his sight returned.

He went to unlock the office door, but it was already open. He noticed splinters of wood and pushed Denise behind him. He turned to her. "Somebody broke in. Call 911, please."

Nine minutes later, Officers Laura Beck and Adam Solomon called them inside.

"Nobody is on the premises, including your apartment, Mr. Conlen." Officer Beck said. "Can you look around and see if anything is missing?"

"Sure, I'll look down here and Denise can look around upstairs."

As he looked through his desk and file cabinets, he didn't notice anything missing. "Everything seems to be here, officers." A moment later he saw Denise coming down the stairs, shaking her head and shrugging her shoulders."

Officer Solomon asked, "When was the last time you were in your office or your apartment?"

"Thursday morning. We took off for a long weekend up in Wrightsville Beach."

"Are you back from your weekend early?" Officer Beck inquired.

Rick shook his head. "No, I got a call from a client that she needed to see me on an urgent matter and it couldn't wait until we returned. She said she needed to see me now, so we drove back. Denise and I have to return to Wrightsville for a dinner engagement this evening.

"So what was so urgent that your client needed to see you in person?" Solomon asked.

He shrugged his shoulders. "Don't know. I haven't told her we had arrived. I was planning on calling her as soon as I got here."

Officer Beck asked, "Can you give us your client's name and number."

"Sure. Her name is Helen Marchant and her number is 910-555-7336."

"When did she call you, Mr. Conlen?"

"I think around seven this morning." He saw a look of concern on Beck's face. "Is something wrong?" He wanted to add that she had the look of someone who just seen a ghost. But then he saw the spirit of Helen Marchant too.

When Solomon saw the translucent figure, he was so shaken he stepped back a couple of steps and fell over a chair in the waiting area, breaking his fall with his right hand, hearing bones snap and crunch. He cried out in pain. Helen Marchant floated over to him and pressed her hand against his wrist and the pain subsided to almost nothing. Solomon's eyes grew wide but she touched him again and his composure returned.

Beck was stunned, but she knew about Conlen being a ghost whisperer from the publicity of last month when the case of a long missing sailor was solved. She turned toward Mrs. Marchant who merely smiled at her.

"Helen, what happened to you?" Denise asked.

"I'd been dead for about nine hours when I called Rick to come back. Walter strangled me and dumped my body down an old well out near LaCosta's farm." She turned toward the police officers. "Do you know where I mean?"

Both of them nodded.

"Anyway, moments after I died, I felt myself leave my body and I could see everything going on around me. Walter tossed me in the dry well, which is very deep, and then he got in his car. I hitched a ride and he came here, jimmied open the door and he searched for something, but he left with nothing, so I can't tell you what he was after."

Out loud, Beck said, "This is absurd, questioning a ghost, but there have been many strange things occurring in this area for quite some time. Why did he kill you?"

"I really don't know. Laura. I thought we had a wonderful life. I came into a large sum of money and we were both able to retire and live nicely. I paid off all the bills, bought Walter a new car and we had the house remodeled. Life was certainly good for several years. He seemed happy all the time. I know an old army buddy died and that bothered him some, but other than that, everything was good."

"Helen, I guess the only way we'll find out is when we find him and bring him in for questioning."

"That will be the easiest part of your job. He's at Eric's Grille having breakfast. Please don't hurt him. I do forgive him, but I certainly want to know why he did it."

The officers put their notebooks away. "We're going to head there now and pick him up. Are you going to allow him to see you, Helen?" Beck asked.

"Perhaps. I'll be around until this matter is all settled, I think?" She looked toward Rick.

"Okay, we'll be in touch. Mr. Conlen and Miss Scott, I guess you can head back to Wrightsville after you secure the office. Ambulock is open so they could probably send someone here in short order."

"Thanks, Officers. I'll get this door secured temporarily and then Denise and I are going to head back to Wrightsville."

After the officers left, Helen, who was now seated, said, "Thanks for coming down. I knew I would not be able to show myself to Laura and Adam without you being present, and I know you are soon going to have your hands full at The Gathering. I didn't want to be called to the island without letting the police know about Walter. There is more to the story than I told them. He had been beating me for years His PTSD has been getting worse for a long time, and even the meds weren't working very well anymore. I don't want him to get a death sentence, so I am asking you to defend him after The Gathering is over. I am beginning to feel a strange sensation. Weird, for a ghost, isn't it. I'm starting to be pulled toward the island. I may not see you there so I am pleading for you to represent Walter. Will you do this for me?"

"Absolutely, Helen. I will defend him to the best of my ability and you needn't worry." For some reason he added, "Go in peace. Serve the Lord."

In a moment she was gone.

An hour later they were on their way back to Wrightsville.

Sunday Evening, July 13th, 2014
Wrightsville Beach, North Carolina.
Masonboro Island, North Carolina

1

Rick and Denise were seated at the South Beach Grill, waiting on the rest of the team. After they ordered drinks, Sam and Sammy were escorted to the table. A few minutes later, the three people Rick had not yet met sat down.

When the waitress, Sherrl Wilhide, came over to take drink orders from the other five people, Rick asked, "Why is there an eighth place setting? I'm not expecting anyone else." He looked at the others, all of whom shrugged their shoulders.

"I don't know, sir, but I'll find out and get right back to you."

Rick saw her talk to the hostess, who was probably looking at a seating chart. She came to the table as Sherrl got the drinks.

"Mr. Conlen, all I know is that I got a call from a man about an hour ago requesting to be seated with you all. He even mentioned you by name, so I had to assume he knows you. If there is any kind of a problem, please let Sherrl or I know and we will rectify the situation."

"Thanks, Miss…."

"Zerbe, Rochelle, please."

"Rochelle, then. I sure don't have any idea who wants to join us, but we look forward to meeting him."

Fifteen minutes passed, allowing everyone to introduce themselves and order another round of drinks. As Denise introduced herself, she saw people get up and walk out of the restaurant, holding their noses and gagging. Some of them were yelling obscenities. She couldn't imagine what was occurring, but a moment later, she caught a whiff of body odor that was stronger than any she had ever smelled, but the odor didn't upset her because there was something about it that was strangely fascinating.

After more people left, she saw the man come toward their table. Some patrons sat back down, ignoring the stench. He was dressed in mismatched, disheveled, visibly dirty clothing. He wore a camouflage sweat soaked baseball cap. His gray beard was matted with vegetation of some kind, and when he smiled, his teeth were obscenely yellow, like that of a long time smoker. Even though he looked and smelled bad, he carried himself tall and proud. He was still about fifteen feet from the table, when he removed his dark sunglasses. She gasped, looking into his incredibly blue eyes. He arrived at the table and stood behind his seat, facing outward. Diners began returning to their seats, and those who had been seated outside, came in. Denise felt that they were in the presence of someone more powerful than they, in the guise of a poor, dirty, old man.

2

Long moments passed before he raised his hands, palms facing up and with that motion, everyone in the restaurant rose as well.

His voice was soft as a whisper, yet powerful as he spoke. "Father, these people, seated at this table, will soon be instruments in your hands. Through them you will finally have your lost souls freed of their earthly chains. However, the dark one, the black angel, will attempt to keep your children from their reward in your kingdom. These soldiers will need your grace and the strength of many more times their number to complete the task you have commissioned. I ask you to grant them the wisdom, the stamina and the time they will need to defeat the enemies of Heaven. For through their perseverance, the spirits of those who never had the opportunity to surrender to you, to move on from the darkness to light. May your will be done on earth as it is in your heavenly kingdom. In the name of the Father, the Son and the Holy Spirit. Amen."

He dropped his hands, and everyone took their seats.

He sat down at the table and took a long drink of water, buttered a small piece of bread and ate it slowly, not being interrupted by anyone. When he finished he said, "If you have any questions to ask of me, please do so, because I will not leave your presence until I am satisfied that all your inquiries are answered. But before that, let us eat and drink our fill."

Sherrl came over to the table and took everyone's orders, promising to have their meals in front of them as quickly as possible.

3

On Masonboro Island, the four humans continued their walks through a sea of spirits. All of them were gleaning information that would help see them through whatever was going to be happening here. They were able to pinpoint the malevolent spirits, finding them in clusters, shying away from the others. They even labeled them, white and dark spirits.

As the sun began its descent to the west, the people started walking back to the campsite. They arrived separately, but within minutes of one another. Mandy was the first one back and although she was still quite shaken after meeting her grandfather, she also felt a sense of calm. She couldn't wait to tell Darrell and she fervently hoped that he, Jason and Maura had also encountered a deceased family member. She just felt that if those happenstances occurred, the four of them would be more at peace, making whatever they were supposed to do, much easier.

She gathered some kindling and after placing the wood shavings in the fire pit, she lit a match to the slivers, seeing them burn quickly. She added some two by fours and then after they started burning, she placed more dry lumber on the fire.. By the time the others were back, the fire was roaring.

Darrell came over to her and gave her a huge hug and a kiss. "Anything exciting happen out there today for you?"

She nodded and invited them all to sit, excitedly telling them about her experience. "How about you guys? Did you run into someone you knew?" Jason and Darrell nodded, but Maura's face was a mask of what appeared to be hate.

"Maura, what happened to you? You seem to be angry and agitated."

Tears filled her eyes and cascaded down her cheeks. Jason held her close and let her cry her heart out. "She had quite an experience out there and if we give her a few moments, she'll share."

A little while later, after she wiped her face and grabbed a beer from the cooler that had been delivered a couple of minutes ago. "I was really quite fascinated with seeing all these earthbound spirits, listening to some of their stories and talking with them. As I spoke to a young woman, who lost her life in an automobile accident in nineteen seventy-seven, I noticed someone approach us from the side. My skin began to crawl as I recognized the man. He had raped me when I was fifteen. I was walking home from school and, stupidly, I must admit, I decide to take a shortcut through an alley. There was garbage strewn about and when I was more than midway through, he came out from a back door, smoking a cigarette and holding a can of beer. I didn't feel threatened because he smiled, nodded and walked away in the opposite direction. Less than a minute later, I was thrown to the street and before I had a chance to scream, he covered my mouth with his big hand."

She took a long pull of her beer, emptying the can and then she reached for another. Everyone noticed that her hand was really shaking badly.

"He said, 'I'm going to take my hand away from your mouth and you are going to come with me or you'll get a lot worse than what I plan to do with you. Do you understand?' I nodded and then I felt the tip of a knife press against my neck. He took his hand away and stood up, motioning me to stand, too. I saw the knife and I was really afraid to scream, figuring he'd kill me right then and there." She began crying again but after a couple of moments and another sip of beer, she continued. "He pushed me toward the door he had come out from and said, 'Open, it and head up the stairs.' I walked up the steps, still trying to figure out a way to save my virginity and my life, but I saw no means of doing either. He told me to stop and then he unlocked the door to an apartment. He pushed me inside and then closed the door behind him. When I turned to face him, I couldn't understand why he wanted to do this. He was a good looking man, about thirty or so, fit looking and dressed nicely. The apartment was neat as a pin and there were pictures on the wall of him with a young woman and two children, a boy and a girl, probably around five or six. All four were smiling in each picture."

Out of the corner of her eye, she saw several spirits approach the campsite. She turned toward them and saw that two men had her attacker constrained with ghostly ropes. She didn't know what to say, but they were apparently bringing him to her. She stood up and screamed. "Why did you bring him here to me? You heard me yell and curse at him until he turned and walked away from me. He died for his crime against me and three other teenage girls and the last thing I want to see again is his face. I was beginning to forget him and what he did to me. Please take him away."

Before they left, one spirit said, "Soon, you will have your opportunity to send him to hell. We just thought you might want to send him there now, but I realize that the time is not yet here." He nodded, turned away and they all walked back to wherever they had come from.

She sat down hard and finished her beer. When she went to get another, Jason, grabbed her hand and shook his head. She nodded and then turned toward the others.

"He took me to the bedroom and made me undress while he watched. I was horrified because I had decided that the first man to see me naked would be my husband. As I took off each article of clothing, I cringed when I saw him smile, leering at me after I took off my bra and as I pulled down my panties he began to rub his crotch. I stood naked in front of him, covering my breasts and my pussy and then he took off his clothes. I gasped when I saw his erection, not believing that it would soon be inside me and I was so afraid that he would hurt me badly. He came over, grabbed me and turned me around, bending me in half and entering me from the rear. I couldn't help but scream my fool head off as he kept thrusting. I heard the knife clatter on the night stand and felt him pull out. It took a moment or two to realize that he had been pulled off of me by two men. They must have heard my scream and came to my aid. One of them tossed me a blanket and I quickly covered myself."

Maura stopped talking again and stared out at the ocean. Nobody dared to speak until they were sure she was finished-she wasn't.

"The two men had been walking down the hallway toward their apartment, when they heard me scream. I remembered I had heard the door open; my attacker apparently forgot to lock it. They called the police and the man was taken away. Months later the case came to trial and the two other teenagers testified as well. The man was sent to prison and I found out he died violently a couple of years ago. It felt so good hearing that and now he's here to haunt me again. I will get great pleasure doing whatever I will have to do to destroy him forever."

Mandy came to her and held her close, both of them crying as the men gave them the time they needed to vent.

After the sun disappeared, the four humans, mentally and physically spent, called it a night.

4

The stranger quietly waited for the first question. He knew what it was going to be, because he heard it many times over the years. He took a sip of water and took a glance at each person at the table.

Sammy asked the question. "Are you God?"

He laughed. "Heavens no, young lady. My name is William Saunders and I am a homeless veteran. I think it is probably my eyes that prompt people to ask that. Of course, when I was younger with dark hair and a dark beard, I was asked if I was Jesus. I did play Him one time when I was in the army. There was a small theater in the town next to the base and I saw an ad looking for actors for a brand new play. No other information was given, but I went to the tryout and won the coveted role of our Lord. After I got out of the military, I grew my hair long and I've been wearing this beard for nearly fifty years."

"Okay, William, or may we call you Bill? What brought you here to our table?" Rick asked.

"Bill is fine, Rick. Actually, a couple of weeks ago, I was ready to move on and head even further south, perhaps Florida, when a young girl approached me. Of course, you all know Hannah by either sight, or by a letter or phone call you may have received from her. She told me she was an angel and that God had a very important assignment for me. She told me to remain where I was until I was contacted again. I was not to eat, nor drink, and not bathe during this time of waiting. She told me that my reward would be the most marvelous gift a person could receive. So I do apologize for my unwashed state. It is pretty hard to say no to God. Of course, you all know that too." He chuckled and when he smiled, his teeth appeared white instead of yellow as they were when he arrived.

There was a very perceptible diminishing of his scent and before their eyes, his clothes began to look cleaner. The dirt on his hands and face was disappearing and his matted beard was beginning to appear whiter and fuller, along with the hair on his head and his eyebrows as well. The creases and crinkles around his eyes reduced and although he was only in his mid-to-late sixties, he looked at least ten years younger than he did just minutes ago.

When Bill saw everyone staring at him and whispering among themselves, he also noticed some of the physical changes they were seeing. His breathing improved and when he took a deep breath, he was able to enjoy the many different scents that are found in a restaurant. That was such a pleasant experience, one that he hadn't had in a great length of time, years, actually. He also felt his insides relaxing. He had been very tight for many years, but now, all the aches and pains he experienced from time to time seemed to be abating. He shrugged his shoulders and rotated his neck around in a circle and he was free of pain in his upper body. Bill thought that his legs felt stronger, but he wouldn't be sure until he stood up and walked around.

Patrons in the restaurant also noticed the air clearing and the changes in Bill. More than one diner believed they were in the presence of God, but they were only in the presence of God's ongoing work. They got back to their meals and their conversations, paying more attention to their table companions than the table where the eight people sat.

The food came and everyone ate with gusto. They enjoyed a goodly amount of wine and beer and Sherrl came to the table carrying a bottle of champagne. "The owner would like you to share this bottle before you leave. I'll bring glasses shortly. Also, there will be no check and he's giving me a double tip and a bonus. Don't ask me why, but I'll take it." She smiled and uncorked the bottle.

After they finished, Bill said, "I don't have a place to stay. Could someone suggest somewhere I might get a room and I also will need some money to pay for my lodging and to either wash my clothes or purchase a new outfit."

Aaron Pammer replied. "Bill you can stay with me. There are two queen size beds in my room, and now I know why they insisted I take that room, at a reduced rate. I have some clothes that will probably fit you pretty well." He smiled.

5

Darrell couldn't sleep, so he headed toward the beach and the campfire that had gone out. He quickly built another one as he listened to the waves rush to shore. In the distance he saw some lightning, but it appeared as though the storm was heading northeast, far away from the island and the mainland too.

He sat down and took a beer from the cooler.

Jason had strolled down to the beach and had a beer too.

"So, after what Maura told us, I guess whatever we had to say would have paled in comparison."

"You're probably right," Jason responded. "It seems like we're seeing people from our past. How about you?"

"A couple of years ago, I lost my best friend. He had a congenital heart problem and he just didn't want to go through the pain of getting a new heart, so he lived every day like it was his last. I always thought I was pretty much of a daredevil, but Alan tried things that I wouldn't even consider. I often witnessed some of his reckless acts. Once he decided to dive off a cliff from at least eighty feet up into the river below. He didn't even know if the water would be deep enough for a dive from that height, so close to the face of the cliff. I looked over the edge after he leaped, praying hard for him to not die. I was able to see him hit the water, and in an instant he disappeared. About two minutes later, he came up grinning from ear to ear, holding on to a fish he must have caught barehanded. He motioned for me to take the dive and I screamed, "No way, Alan. You're a fucking idiot, you know."

Jason laughed. "Yeah, I sure as hell took some chances too, probably most of them fueled by alcohol." He shook his head. "Didn't know I'd get all the thrills a man could ever want in Afghanistan...." He grew quiet and Darrell knew not to say anything, just to wait until his flashback passed, hopefully without Jason flipping out.

"So what else did Alan do?" Jason asked after grabbing two more beers and handing one to Darrell.

"Well, he went on every rollercoaster he could find. I never had the balls to go on them things and I don't consider myself a weenie, but height is one thing that gets me; sometimes makes me sick to my stomach, although I love flying. Go figure. Anyway, couple of years ago he bought himself a classic car, a '69 Dodge Super Bee with a 440 six pack, four speed with only 22 thousand miles. Paid 67 grand for it. He heard about a drag race place and figured he could beat anyone in the world with that car. It was really fast, Jason, and the man shifted that sucker so quick and smooth, hardly even felt it going into a different gear. I drove it once and it was love, man."

"He left for the drag race one day a couple of weeks later and he never came back. All I ever found out was that his car exploded, but I never knew how until earlier today when I saw him up near the north end of the island. Alan was shredded and the only way I knew him was by his voice when he talked to me. He told me he tried a new mix of gas and a couple of chemicals that when they mixed were supposed to burn so fast, giving him a quicker jump off the line. He said it worked great until he had the RPMs up to eight thousand and when he shifted gears, the car just blew up. He said he never even felt himself burn, nor car parts pass through his face and body. He figured that being earthbound was his punishment for being such an asshole, and he is looking forward to leaving here, no matter where he winds up. Hope God wants him, Jason. He was a good man, even if a little crazy. So how about you? Want another beer?"

"Yeah, thanks." Darrell handed him a cold Yuengling Lager and he drained it in only a couple of swallows. "I killed a fellow soldier and today I saw him again." Jason turned toward his friend. Darrell was leaning toward the fire and his expression, or rather, lack of one, told Jason that Darrell was not going to judge him, at least until he heard the entire story. He waited until

Darrell added a couple of boards to the fire before he continued.

"We were out on a mission and just before dark we set in for the night on top of a sand dune. We all dug out shallow pits to lie in, deep enough that we were below the surface of the sand, offering some protection from small arms. It would take a direct hit on top of me to blow me away. There were six of us and we were all tired from the general army bullshit, the heat, the country, and nearly anything else one could think of. I guess we probably all dozed off at one time or another during the night. When I did, I had no idea how long I had been asleep, or if anyone at all was awake, but when I woke up, I heard movement out in front of my hole. It sounded like someone was crawling right toward me and I was scared shitless." Jason stopped and lit a cigarette with shaking hands, allowing Darrell to see the fear in his eyes as he told his story.

"I was lying on my back. I guess I flipped over in my sleep, which I rarely did since joining the army, but I didn't want to turn over and make any unnecessary noise. I slowly removed my knife from the sheath tied to my chest and steeled myself for hand to hand combat, hoping that my opponent wouldn't be ready for it. A moment later, I saw his silhouette slithering beside my hole. I waited for an opportune moment and leapt up rolling on top of him, stabbing him repeatedly. I heard a gasp and then there was nothing. I don't think anyone heard the killing, even though my heart was hammering so loudly. When dawn broke, I saw that what I thought was an enemy soldier was an American dressed in shorts and a dark t-shirt, his head bandaged heavily. The bandage was bloody. I searched him for paperwork, just as the other guys were waking up. I found his ID and when the others saw him and asked what happened, I told them. "I didn't know he was one of us, guys. What am I going to do?" They all decided to bury the guy and nobody would ever say anything. I thought the dude was a raghead, Darrell. Swear to God. I've lived with this for a long time and haven't been able to get it out of my head. Today when I saw him he told me he forgave me because he was the stupid one. He got separated from his unit and fell, gashing his head. He wrapped it in some rags he found lying about and just started walking toward what he thought was his base camp. He slept for a while, but after dark, he began his trek again, and that's when I killed him. He had been sleeping less than twenty-five yards in front of our position. He never heard us digging in. I think once we get off this island, I'm going to the nearest army facility and tell them my story. I only hope that the other guys from the squad won't have to be punished, but since they were accessories, I imagine they will be."

"Don't worry too much, Jason. I'm sure we'll be able to find an attorney to take your case. You couldn't have possibly known the guy was an American and you certainly couldn't have asked him either. Maybe we better get back to the girls and get some sleep, now."

Jason nodded. "Thanks, man. It feels good getting that off my chest."

6

Back at the hotel, Bill felt great after spending thirty-five minutes in the shower. He hadn't taken one in so long he had almost forgotten how good hot water could feel. He toweled off and looked at himself in the full length mirror on the back of the door. His body was leaner and firmer than it had been in many years. God had given him a gift for sure. He felt a good twenty years younger, even though his age still showed somewhat. He wondered if he would be able to recapture some of his youth in the near future, hopefully lasting for some time to come.

Aaron's clothes, for now consisting of a Harley t-shirt and grey Bermuda shorts, fit him pretty well and he couldn't wait to get some new clothes and perhaps find a job somewhere. He felt he would be able to do anything now and he was truly tired of living the life he had been living for way too long.

He didn't know what was in store for him tomorrow, but whatever it was, he would do the best he could.

He stepped out from the bathroom and saw Aaron watching TV. "Aaron, my new friend. I feel really good. Could I impose upon you to take me out for a couple of beers?"

"That sounds pretty good, Bill. I don't think we should stay out too late because Rick wants us to have a good breakfast together tomorrow. He wants to leave around quarter to six, so let's have a couple and then get a good night's sleep."

Monday Morning, July 14th, 2014
Wilmington, North Carolina
Masonboro Island, North Carolina

1

At six AM, eight people were seated at a long table inside the Causeway Café. There were some smiles and small talk, but overall the mood was somber. Coffee was sliding down parched throats, since everyone was nervous about the events yet to occur.

After a long silence, Rick decided they needed to talk about what Hannah and George might have planned for them. "We have about forty-five minutes before we have to head down to the river. I'm sure all of us have some kind of concerns and now would be the time to share them because I think once we're given our instructions, we need to be both physically and mentally prepared. Denise and I run almost every day, we go to the gym and try to keep ourselves as fit as possible. Sure, there are times we eat wrong and drink too much, but when that happens we get right back to our routines and in a short period of time, we're as strong as we can be. So, is there anyone who feels he or she is not fit enough to handle running, climbing, crawling and whatever exertion we might have to put out to complete the mission?"

He took a sip of water and loaded his fork with grits and shrimp, rapidly putting the food in his mouth and barely chewing it at all before he swallowed. He looked at everyone, each for several seconds, trying to read their faces, but to no avail. Each person at the table was as expressionless as a mannequin in a department store. No smiles, no frowns, nothing, and that had him a little worried.

Bill cleared his throat, mainly to get everyone's attention. "I'm the oldest of the group and my lifestyle hasn't been the best for a very long time. After I got out of the army, I was in damn good shape. I could run ten miles with a full pack on my back and an M-16 in my hand. The toughest thing I faced when returning to civilian life was fitting in. My old friends avoided me like the plague. Hell, some of them didn't even know I was a Vietnam vet. I remember one of my high school friends coming up to me at a bar asking me where I had been because he hadn't seen me in a long time. When I told him I just came back from a year in Vietnam, he called me an asshole and a baby killer and spilled his beer over my head. I so wanted to strangle him then and there, but I knew it wouldn't do any good. I headed to New York to try to get some work in plays and two times I was an extra in a movie being shot. I wasn't making very much money and every time I brought up Vietnam, more people shied away from me. I headed south and wound up here in Wilmington, getting day jobs, living in a cheap, dirty hotel. It was all I could afford, but after about twenty years of that, I just grew tired of everything and I've been living on the street ever since. I did take long walks every day because there wasn't much else to do. There were times I walked up to fifteen miles a day. I was always fortunate to get enough food to keep myself going and keep me strong, so even at my age, I do believe I'll be able to handle whatever physical exertion we'll have to perform." He went back to his breakfast.

A man seated directly behind Bill, turned around and tapped him on the shoulder. When Bill turned to him, the man said, "I couldn't help overhearing your conversation. I am a Vietnam vet too and I am one of the lucky ones. I never saw combat, but I saw the aftereffects of war and that always stuck with me. When I came home, I wanted to forget everything, but I kept running into guys and gals who served there too. I decided I needed to do something for vets, so I started up a business, providing courier services. I franchised the business out and my company can be found in all fifty states. The only prerequisite to being in my employ is to be a veteran. If you don't have a criminal record, I'll give you a job and we'll start from there." He handed Bill his card. "I don't know what your plans are for now, but if you're interested in earning a decent living, give me a call and we'll talk." The man, Larry Stevens, turned back to his female companion, actually his wife, and resumed eating his breakfast.

The entire group heard the conversation and those closest to him patted Bill on the back while the rest raised their water glasses to salute him.

Bill was stunned, never thinking he would have an opportunity to turn his life around, but he would certainly give Larry a call as soon as he could.

Shortly after the sun popped up from the ocean, Jason and Maura rebuilt the fire. There were eggs in the cooler, so once the fire was hot, Sammy broke them all into a large bowl, stirred them with a fork and put them into a skillet that was heating up on the grill plate several inches above the burning lumber. Sam filled the aluminum coffee pot with water and coffee and placed it beside the skillet. It wasn't long before the scent of both eggs and coffee awakened Darrell and Mandy.

A couple of minutes later, the eggs and coffee were being enjoyed by the four people and as they ate, ghosts were popping up everywhere, almost as if they had been asleep as well. However, none of the people knew whether ghosts needed to rest or were they always awake.

A spirit, once a middle aged man with a huge weight problem, strolled up to the fire. He tried to grab a plate but his hand just kept passing through the red plastic dish. He next tried to pick up a blue plastic coffee cup to no avail. "Damn, this being dead really sucks. I haven't had eggs and coffee in over eighty years, but I never stop trying." He looked at the foursome and said, "Guess I won't have to worry about it much longer though, word is that there are more people coming here later and they have the means to send us to Heaven or Hell. I still am not sure where I'll wind up, but, like I said, eighty years of this is more than enough for me."

They watched him walk back toward the center of the island, and suddenly, he stopped, threw his hands up in the air, and spoke something that could not be heard. He dropped his arms down until his body took the shape of a cross. A moment later, he smiled as he was lifted straight off the ground and floated upward until he could no longer be seen.

Darrell had grabbed his iPhone and filmed the entire incident. After the man disappeared from view, he stopped the video and then replayed it. Everything he had seen was captured but he was astonished when the video showed two nearly invisible entities pushing his outstretched arms upward.

He showed the video to his friends and they were astounded as well.

3

Promptly at 8 AM, the eight new friends stood on the wooden sidewalk looking across the Cape Fear River at the great old battleship. The North Carolina saw a lot of action in its day. As the first newly built battleship put into service in World War II, she saw action in every major engagement in the Pacific theater. She served with distinction for over six years, and in 1962, she was turned into a museum.

They stared at her for a lengthy time, seeing figures scurrying around on the deck, on top of the superstructure and sitting on guns and the airplane's wings. Some waved, while others cupped their hands around their mouths, probably trying to antagonize those who would soon be aboard her, ridding her forever of spirits.

Rick heard a lot about her over the time he'd lived in Southport and it was reported that there were only two spirits haunting the ship; one malevolent and one peaceful and shy. He certainly knew that someone was feeding the general public a crap sandwich, probably to keep people coming. He figured if he was a visitor and heard there were only two spirits on board, he could deal with it. Already Rick counted nine ghosts and he figured there were more in the bowels of the ship. And then again, perhaps visitors were given that information because only two had ever been seen.

A couple of minutes later, Hannah arrived and everyone turned toward her, hoping to hear that this was all a joke and they could all go home.

She smiled at them and then said. "Thank you all for coming. As you all saw, there are many more than two spirits on board the North Carolina. They have learned the art of hiding, sometimes in plain sight, but you should be able to send them all on their way in a short period of time. Does everyone have a squirt gun, a bottle of water and a pair of glasses, and have each other's cell phone numbers?"

They all nodded but Bernadette raised her hand. "I'm sure you're going to tell us the purpose of these items, but may I venture a guess?"

"You certainly may. What do you think these items are for?"

"I think the water that you provided is special and when used to fill the squirt guns, we will be able to shoot them and that action will allow them to shed their earthbound chains and journey to where their final reward awaits. I haven't been able to figure out the glasses, though."

"She is correct. You are each to carry a bottle filled with holy water at all times, in order to refill your squirt guns. The glasses will allow you to determine which spirits are still in darkness and which are in light."

Kyle raised his hand, as though in school and Hannah was the teacher.

"Yes, Kyle. You have a question?"

"I do. There are only eight of us here, yet there are 12 of each item. What are the other four for?"

Hannah looked to her left, at nothing there, and after what seemed to be a few minutes of listening to nobody, she turned back to Kyle. "George said that you will know the reason for the other four sets of items in due time. So, I'm sorry but I cannot answer that question. Any other questions before I give you your instructions?"

The group was silent, so Hannah said, "Very well. George has seen to giving you all two hours aboard the battleship, with no interruptions of any kind. You are to stay in pairs at all times and when you see a spirit, squirt it. They will appear to dissolve before your eyes, and you will also be able to see if they are being sent to Heaven or to Hell. The water taxi behind you will take you to and return you from the ship. We will meet again after you have completed your mission." She vanished.

4

They climbed aboard the water taxi and paired up. Rick and Denise, Kyle and Bernadette, Sam and Sammy, and Bill and Aaron. They watched as the battleship grew larger. After docking, they boarded the ship, fanning out to cover the deck, gun turrets and the superstructure first.

After donning the glasses, Aaron felt like his regular vision improved tenfold. He saw people on the other side of the river, going about their business. He could see their lips move when they were talking to their companions or on a Bluetooth. He could even read signs posted along the walkway and he was hoping he would be allowed to keep these marvelous glasses forever.

The others were experiencing similarities with their eyesight, especially Rick. He was truly amazed with the great distance he could see, not only the people, but their features as well, right down to the creases on their faces and the hair on men's arms. The glasses they were all wearing were truly gifts from God.

Sam was the first to spot a spirit hiding inside a 40mm gun turret, trying to blend with the gray metal. It looked pitiful. What was once a man, full of life and dreams for the future, was now just a shadow of his former life. His lips were moving but there was no sound, although Sam was close enough to feel air rushing from his mouth. He wished he could read lips, but learning that had never been on his bucket list.

From her vantage point ten feet away from her brother and the spirt, Sammy aimed her iPhone, capturing the ghost's one sided conversation. She had the ability to read lips and was fascinated with what the spirit was saying. His eyes were as pleading as his words.

Although Sam didn't understand what the spirt was saying, he figured it wouldn't hurt to let him ramble on. The ghost only spoke for a short length of time and when he finished, he stood up and later Sam would have sworn that the ghost puffed up his chest. Sam lifted his lime green squirt gun and aimed at the ghost's chest. He pulled the trigger and was shocked when he felt a slight recoil as the needle size jet of water spat from the front of the barrel. As though in slow motion, perhaps another feature of the glasses, Sam actually saw the water hit the spirit in the chest, knocking it backward and lifting it off its feet before the figure literally dissolved, as though it was made out of water too. Of course, the human body was comprised of about seventy percent water, so that kind of made sense in a situation that made no sense at all. Even though his faith had returned, he was still a little perplexed with this whole mission, but he would continue on to the finish, trusting in God.

"That was awesome, Sam," she said and then he turned toward her.

"Yeah, it was. I would have never believed a squirt gun could be so powerful. But, I guess when God gives you something to use, it's going to be pretty good. How long have you been here?"

"Long enough to get a video of the spirit talking to you and it will probably take a little while but I think I can tell you every word he said."

He nodded. "He sure was trying to get a lot out before I sent him away."

Over the course of the next few minutes, Sammy told her brother everything the spirit said. "Okay, his name was Sylvester Ottolini and he served aboard the ship during the war. When he came home, he thought he was fine, but over the course of the next few years, he'd remember a mission and see it in his mind's eye. He was happy that no one got killed anywhere near him, but remembering the sights and sounds of battle just wore on him every day. Twelve years after the war ended, one of his best buddies passed away. They had been in contact and got together a couple of times a year. Willie Cafera was wounded during the Marianas Turkey Shoot and over the years his pain grew worse until he just couldn't handle it anymore and he ate a bullet. Sylvester said that once his friend passed, his nightmares worsened and he drank like crazy until he took the same road to having peace back in ninety-seven. He never even left a note for his wife, Verna. He asked you to please contact her, she lives in Hyannisport on Cape Cod and he wants you to tell her he was sorry that he had to end his life, but he just couldn't live with his memories anymore. He wants you to tell her he loved her very much and that he was looking forward to seeing her in Heaven. He even told you the date she's going to die; her last day will be October 17th, 2017, so she's going to have a couple more years before she joins him."

She placed her hands on his shoulders and in a soft voice said, "Sam, I hope I never know the day I'm going to die because I'm afraid I would change the way I live and I don't ever want to do that. We denied ourselves for so long because of our anger and we need to make up for that time and tell people about how wonderful having faith in God can be."

Sam nodded and then he and his sister heard yelling on the other side of the ship. The started racing toward the sound.

Kyle and Bernie, as she now wanted to be called, were sweeping the area around the airplane that was welded to a stand on the deck. Kyle saw a ghost playing peekaboo with him, kinda slithering around the fuselage from one side to another. He looked over his shoulder and it appeared as though Bernadette was having a conversation with a ghost dressed in Navy whites. He looked like he was an officer in life and he figured he'd get a chance to hear the spirit's story after he finished playing tag with this one. He turned his attention back to the plane and then saw that the ghost, dressed in Navy dungarees had taken refuge on the top of the crane. Kyle raised his lime green squirt gun and took aim. He had no idea how far it would shoot, but it certainly couldn't hurt to try. He fired and saw the jet of water head toward the target, but just before it would have hit the specter in the right leg, the bastard moved, really fast and Kyle missed.

Kyle approached the crane, figuring he'd climb up and shoot the ghost at closer range. He found footholds and handholds and when he was near the top of the vertical part of the structure, he saw the ghost sitting at the far end of the horizontal part of the crane. Just when Kyle was ready to start climbing out to the end, where the ghost was sitting, he felt a tug on the back of his belt, he was lifted off of the crane and began to swing madly back and forth. He screamed and tried to keep his arms as close to his body as possible so as not to jar himself loose from whatever was attached to his belt. He turned his head around looking for a wire or a cable and found nothing. He had a moment when he felt that he wasn't going to hit anything with his body and discovered that there was nothing holding him, or that whatever it was, was invisible. He became frightened with the prospect of falling and possibly be subjected to life in a wheelchair again. He clawed at the air, trying to grab something solid to stop the maddening ride and he screamed for all he was worth.

Bernie turned away from the ghost she was talking with and scampered toward the crane, seeing her new friend basically flying back and forth and spinning around with no visible means of support. She didn't know what to do or how to end his agonizing ride. She just hoped that if he fell, she would be able to catch him somehow before he hit the wooden deck or was thrown out over the river and then released. He just kept yelling and it was beginning to get on her nerves.

Sam and Sammy arrived and both of them assessed the situation and began climbing the crane. Sam was hanging on to the horizontal portion of the crane and trying to grab Kyle with his legs, hoping to scissor him and stop his wild ride. Sammy was trying to grab him as he swung near her and one time she almost had him in her grasp.

Moments later the remaining members of the team arrived at the crane. Bill watched the action and thought that if this was not a serious situation, the whole thing could be pretty damn funny. He had an idea though. He recruited Aaron, Rick and Denise and told them what he needed. They all hurried down the ladders until they came to a sleeping area. They each grabbed a mattress and struggled getting them back up to the deck, but eventually the four mattresses were laid out side by side under the area where Kyle was swinging. The four team members on the deck aimed their squirt guns just above Kyle's head, pulled the triggers and didn't let go. Jets of water flew toward the invisible wire until finally it was cut. Kyle fell straight down and landed on the mattresses but he bounced onto the deck, cracking his right elbow. He screamed bloody murder until Bill soothed him and popped the bone back into place easing Kyle's pain greatly.

When he stood up, he saw the ghost sitting near the end of the crane, silently clapping his hands and laughing. He seemed so happy that he caused a human pain and this angered Kyle.

Kyle began walking away and then turned quickly, aiming his squirt gun toward the spirit, and then fired three jets of holy water in rapid succession. He saw the ghost's eyes grow wide just as the first water bullet struck him under the chin, turning his head and then his entire body into something like water vapor and the ghost was gone.

Bill watched in fascination and exclaimed, "Holy crap, Kyle that was so much like a scene in the movie *Rio Bravo*, where the deputy sheriff, Dude, played by Dean

Martin, figured out that the outlaw he had wounded outside the saloon was hiding in the rafters after he saw blood dripping into a beer glass on the bar. Dude started walking away, turned and fired, I think two shots, and the man fell to the floor dead. That was remarkable shooting, man!"

"Thanks," Kyle said, blowing on the barrel of the squirt gun as though smoke was coming from it, and then put it in his pocket, much like returning a pistol to its holster."

Everyone laughed, but then the mood grew serious again. They discussed how they were going to clear the entire ship of ghosts. Bill and Aaron would stay topside, keeping their eyes peeled on the entrance to the lower levels, while everyone else would head down to the bottom and start working their way back up. Hopefully every area would be covered because there were many hatchways and ladders to navigate to search the entire ship bottom to top.

Sam and Sammy decided to go to the engine room first because that was the lowest level they could get to. They hoped that there were no spirits hiding in the areas not open to visitors and if possible they would search those places too. When they arrived in the engine room, they were bewildered by the mass of pipes, wires, valves and gauges they saw. Sam went to the left and Sammy to the right, covering every possible hiding space they could find. Sam saw a long dead sailor hiding in between two pipes. He said, "Are you ready to see God?" The spirit nodded, smiled and crawled from the tiny area, giving Sam a full body shot. Sam took it and like the others, felt a recoil that should have never been present when firing a squirt gun, but these were the Lord's weapons, much more powerful than those made by man.

The spirit disappeared into a small pool of wetness on the metal floor, and moments later that was gone too. He was certain he saw the vapor rise, showing that the spirit was going to be accepted in heaven.

Sammy found a target lying on the floor under where the commodes had once been in the engine room bathroom. She didn't even attempt to coax him out, like she saw her brother do, and she certainly wasn't going to ask him anything. As she aimed, she felt like she was going to be a killer, even though the person was long dead, only leaving behind a mere shadow of himself, sometimes three dimensionally, but the ones she had seen so far, only had width and height. One shot sent him on a downward spiral.

They swept the remainder of the level, seeing nothing, but they actually were enjoying seeing the guts of a ship that fought in great battles seventy years ago and more. They were ready to move upward again.

Rick and Denise headed down a number of ladders, the last being a spiral type and arrived in the section where the big guns' shells were stored. Many were on a conveyer system to be fed upward to the banks of weapons. The pair couldn't even begin to count how many were there on display and how much firepower this battleship was capable of producing all those years ago. There were hundreds of bags of powder that would be loaded in the breech behind the big shell and when ignited would propel the round out through the barrel to targets up to many miles away.

Denise never let her eyes stop moving. She felt the hairs on the back of her neck stand up and she was certain a very evil spirit was somewhere in this compartment. As she did a visual sweep, she caught the slightest motion of something that had nearly blended in with a white cardboard cutout of a sailor with an arrow sign affixed to the front signifying the direction of the tour. She kept staring at it just to make sure that she wasn't seeing things and moments later she saw a ghostly head peer out from behind the cardboard sailor. She was unwavering as she slowly raised her black squirt gun and then her hand moved swiftly, bringing the weapon to bear on the spirit. She pulled the trigger and held it for a very short time, but time enough to fire four holy water bullets. Three of them found their mark and the spirit dissolved, scowling at her for ending its earthbound existence. The spirt was on its way to Satan's dominion. She felt good with her first 'kill' and knew she would be ready for anything.

Rick saw a spirit darting behind a row of shells lining a wall. He led it with his squirt gun and when he saw an opening, he fired. The jet of water hit the ghost in the right arm and spun him around. He kept running, finally dissolving into a pool of water on the metal floor. Rick smiled, knowing he had done a good job sending this spirit to its final reward. He felt good when he saw the vapor was Heaven bound because he looked like a kid, probably no more than eighteen or nineteen when he died. He didn't know what the spirit's connection was to the battleship, because he wasn't wearing a uniform of any kind.

Denise was still checking out the area and when she heard something behind her, she spun and fired her squirt gun hitting Sammy slightly below the waist.

Sammy looked down where the water bullet hit and saw wetness, but there was no pain, so she deduced that humans couldn't be harmed by the holy water in the squirt guns.

Denise lowered her gun and said, "Oh, Sammy! I'm so sorry. This ship is starting to give me the creeps and I'll be happy when we are done here. Did you guys run into any ghosts?"

"Yeah, we did. Each of us sent one on its way, one up and one down. How about you and Rick?"

As she saw Rick approaching she nodded her head. "We each got one and then searched the area thoroughly. Didn't see any more."

"It seems as though we are only allowed to send one spirit on its way. You guys think this is just a test for us to see how well we handle ourselves?" Sam said.

"You might have something there, Sam," Rick replied. "Kyle got one, and we all did, so that leaves Bill, Aaron and, uh, I'm not sure if Bernie got one, but I'm guessing we can probably head back up and go out on the deck. Unless a couple of ghosts are going to force them to a lower level, my bet is that the remainder of lost souls will be waiting for us topside."

"I think you could be right, Rick," Denise replied. "Let's head up and see what's going on. This place does give me the creeps."

As they strolled back through the kitchen to the ladder that would take them to the deck, a couple of ghosts took the ladder first and wound up outside, heading right toward Bill and Aaron.

Bill saw them first and yelled to Aaron. "Two are up here on deck, buddy. Guess it's our turn to do some shooting."

Aaron nodded and followed one that was beginning to head up the superstructure. He quickly fell in behind the spirit, not letting him out of his sight. He saw the ghost head onto the bridge and when he arrived there, he looked all around, but the spirit was nowhere to be found. He walked over to the round windows that circled the room and looked out over the deck of the ship, seeing Bill standing down there doing nothing. He was just standing like a statue causing Aaron to wonder if he was okay. Suddenly he heard a whispering sound and when he turned toward the captain's chair, he saw the ghost sitting there as though he had done it many times before.

The spirit was probably about five feet eight inches and he wore thick glasses. He opened his mouth and spoke slowly. "I know what you must now do and I accept my fate. There are many of us and few of you, so your work will not be easy. My name is Ron Mazzaro and I was a radio operator during the war on this ship. I died in 1987, almost forty years to the day after the North Carolina was decommissioned. I don't know how my spirit arrived aboard the ship because I was in Connecticut, near my home, keeping watch over my daughter and her husband. I don't know who will watch over them now because soon I will be gone. I hope God knows what he's doing by removing us from earth because I think there is a need for us to remain. That's all I have to say, so do what you must."

Aaron pulled the trigger and watched the spirit dissolve into a small puddle on the chair. Moments later, the puddle turned into vapor and he watched it evaporate in an upward motion, so he figured Ron was on his way to Heaven. Ron's message troubled him somewhat but only for a minute or two and then he heard laughter and his name was being shouted out, so he returned to the deck.

When he returned to the deck, he said, "What's going on? You guys were laughing like you heard the funniest joke ever."

Bill said, "Kyle asked Bernie what she and her ghost were in animated conversation about and then he said, well, why don't we let her tell you." He started laughing again.

Bernie smiled and tried to stop laughing herself, but even after hearing the story once and repeating it to everyone already, she still couldn't stop. Finally after a couple of bursts of laughter, she settled down and said, "My ghost was a cook on board the ship and he wanted to come clean with something he did once, when he was a small game and deer hunter before the war began. He hunted regularly with a group of eight, including himself. The group consisted of his dad, his uncle, three cousins, one who became an admiral, his best friend, Adam Lerch and Adam's younger brother, John."

She started giggling again and she had to calm herself down before continuing. "Anyway, Henry, my ghost, drew the short straw that week and he was responsible for cooking dinner every night. He tried to make some really good meals, but he had a lot of trouble with seasoning everything. Adam constantly bitched about everything Henry cooked and by the fourth night of the two week camp, Henry had had enough, especially of Adam's favorite comment when he didn't like something. Well that night was burger night, so Henry had a plan. He told everyone what he was going to do and they all agreed that it would probably be the funniest prank ever."

Now the others were coming down with screaming giggles, knowing what was coming and she had to stop again. As soon as the laughter stopped she continued.

"When the guys came back from town, a necessary beer run, the plan had already been set in place. Adam, his brother and Henry's uncle put away the groceries and the beer, as the others took their seats at the table. "Okay guys, anyone complains about the burgers will be cooking dinner for the rest of our time here, because I have had it," Henry told them. He brought the burgers over and put one on each bun. When he got to Adam, he gave him the special burger, made solely for him. All the guys fixed their burgers, adding onions, mustard, ketchup, slices of cheese, chatting about the day. Adam looked at his and sniffed it. It smelled different, but he seemed to be the only one to notice something odd. The other guys were devouring theirs, so he spread some ketchup and mustard on the bun, added a slice of cheese, put it together and took a bite. He spit it out after chewing it, gagging and making faces. He looked at Henry with hatred in his eyes and screamed, "This burger tastes like shit" When he saw the others starting to smile, he added, "But good." The guys just lost it and couldn't stop laughing, knowing that Adam hated cooking and didn't want to have that responsibility at all. Of course, he was not made to finish his dinner, but he never complained again.

Aaron was almost crying, he was laughing so hard. "Wow that was really a good one." He forgot to tell the others what happened on the bridge.

"Yeah, I thought I'd pee myself when he told me, but he said that was the only bad thing he ever did in his life, so he just wanted me to know that before I squirted him. He was on his way up to Heaven moments later."

Soon they heard a boat pull into the dock and they left the ship. When they were all aboard, Hannah appeared to them and said, "Good job, everyone. You passed the test and now you are going to be taken to Masonboro Island. There you will meet up with four more people and the twelve of you will clear the island of the remainder of the earthbound ghosts. Many will beg you to let them stay on earth, but no matter what they tell you, you must not let them sway you from your mission. I will see you again soon." She disappeared.

They took an inventory of the items on the boat. There were two coolers filled with ice and beer. There were several bottles of wine in another, along with bottled water and some soda. A waterproof bag contained snacks. There was an empty one for the squirt guns, the bottles of water that were once again filled to the top, and the glasses. Bill volunteered to carry that one to land.

When they were near the island, they were told to inflate the rafts, load the supplies and paddle to shore.

Monday, July 14th, 2014
Masonboro Island

1

The two couples on the beach watched as eight people entered the two inflatable rafts and then pulled coolers, beach chairs and other items on board and started paddling toward shore.

When the rafts were less than fifty feet from shore, a larger than usual wave crested behind them. The onshore party started waving and pointing, but the only response they got was that a few of the people waved back, pretty much oblivious to the six foot tall wall of water that was going to crash down on them at any moment.

Darrell and Jason quickly slipped out of their sandals and rushed toward the ocean. Just as they hit the water, running full bore, the wave rolled over the rafts, tossing people and items from the rubber boats, lifting the rafts high in the air. When they landed, they began to wash back away from the beach.

The two swimmers managed to get to the victims in short order, seeing that all of them appeared okay. The items they carried with them in the rafts were quickly floating away, save for a large canvas bag. An older man, sporting white hair and a matching beard, held it tightly to his body.

"Are you all okay?" Darrell shouted out once the water calmed down again and they'd be able to hear him.

He got a thumbs up from the eight people in the water and as he looked south, he saw Jason swimming with one arm, holding on to a large cooler. He had a waterproof bag around his neck, resting on his back and another one draped over his shoulder. Darrell just shook his head wondering how Jason managed to retrieve all that stuff in the short time they were out there.

About fifteen minutes later, everyone and everything that could be found was hauled in to shore. One raft didn't make it and the group saw it drifting farther and farther from the beach, heading south.

They stared at Bill, and Mandy said, "Are you...?"

He said, "God?" Then he explained why people thought that.

When Bill finished his story, Mandy and Maura helped to make the newcomers comfortable. Wet clothing was replaced with spare clothing they and the guys had. Unfortunately not everyone could wear some of the offered clothing and elected to sit around in towels waiting for their clothes to dry. The day was hot and the wind was blowing at a pretty good clip, so it probably wouldn't take too long for them to get dressed again.

The girls served beer, wine, water, soda and snacks to the hungry and thirsty people, allowing them time to regenerate their bodies before the deluge of questions they would have for them.

About an hour later, they saw a large contingent of ghosts walk toward the beach, studying the new strangers. Some of them appeared to be communicating with one another and there was much finger pointing and animated motion with hands and arms.

"Whoa! How many ghosts are on this island, Maura?" Aaron said after seeing what appeared to be at least one hundred spirits of both sexes, of various ages, and from the clothing they wore, from many time periods.

'I don't know for sure, Aaron, but the four of us have seen probably thousands as we walked around the island. The island isn't too wide but it is almost eight miles long and there are many areas that one just can't walk in too easily because of the marshland. I still don't know what we're supposed to be doing here, but I imagine one of you guys or gals will tell us when the time is right."

After Maura finished, Rick stood up. "What we're all here for is to send all the spirits on this island to either Heaven or Hell. God has assigned us the mission and we didn't know that any more people would be here at all. Now that there are twelve of us, it makes me wonder if we are to become the twelve new apostles. I don't think our mission will be completed once we finish here."

He heard the gasps from the four who had been on the island for a couple of days already.

Sam stood up. "My sister, Sammy and I lost our parents when we were twelve and our faith in God had ended that day. I never thought we would ever get it back, but when we saw a vison of our mother, she told us we needed to come here and that our lives would change forever. I think Rick is right. This isn't the last thing God has planned for us."

Aaron said, "I was a terrible stutterer and thought I would have to suffer with that all my life. Actually, the past few years have been the worst and it got to the point where I was often too embarrassed to even speak at all. Photography became my passion because when I had a camera in my hands, even if I was pretending to shoot something or someone, I didn't have to verbally communicate to anyone. After seeing and shooting what I saw on Friday, my stuttering disappeared. I can thank God for curing me, but I didn't know if I'd be ready for what he wants me to do now, or in the future."

Bernadette said, "I suffered from a horrible skin disease from birth. I tried to fit in with all my friends, but you know how kids are, they just beat you up verbally when you're different. It was a rough go for many years but getting a job on the Midway was a really good thing for me. I was earning a living and saw very few people during my night shift duty. I looked up everything I could find concerning my skin condition, hoping that there might be a treatment that could help me look a little more normal, but there was nothing. When I touched the ghost plane, I just felt a tingle throughout my body and soon after, I was healed. I was back to normal. There is no way I can repay God for the gift he has given me, but I will do anything He asks of me, no matter how often nor how long the assignment will last." She cracked a smile filled with joy and happiness."

Kyle stood up and walked to a cooler, grabbing a beer. After a couple of swallows, he told his story. "It wasn't easy getting around in a wheelchair, so when I saw the Mexican army heading toward the Alamo, I went as fast as I could in my permanent ride. When I hit something and fell off, I was scared shitless, but then Jesus helped me up and I ran to the Alamo. I couldn't wait to get to Wilmington and get on board the North Carolina." He laughed. "Of course, I never thought I'd be swinging around on an invisible cable either. I don't think it was coincidence that the cable snapped when I was just about perfectly straight above the mattresses that were placed on the deck under me. I am resigned to do all I have to do to finish this work and get back home to Texas. I have a lot of things I want to do there to thank a bunch of people for the help they gave me all these years." Kyle took a long swallow of beer and then let out a great belch to the laughter of all the others.

Rick told them about his blindness and Jason revealed his inner ghosts. The only ones who seemed not to have any issues or impairments were Darrell, Mandy and Denise. It was interesting that not everyone gathered here hadn't suffered from something, but their lack of former disabilities were not even a concern among the twelve humans on this island.

Several minutes of uncomfortable silence followed, the quiet broken by Kyle. "So what is the plan, gang. How are we going to end the earthbound existence of thousands of ghosts? It's going to take quite a bit of time to do this."

"My thought was we'd start at the southern tip of the island and work our way northward. We probably won't get the job done today, and maybe not even by sunset tomorrow, but we gotta start somewhere." Rick answered. He said, "Anyone have a better idea?"

When no one responded, he stood up and said, "Okay, let's get to it, then, and see how far we get. We have a good seven hours of light ahead of us, so the sooner we start, the more we can accomplish." He told

Bill to give everyone a squirt gun, water and glasses and Jason erupted in laughter.

"Really, Rick! We're going to shoot ghosts with these?"

Rick saw a ghost forty to fifty yards down the beach. He took aim, allowing for drop and sent out a couple of jets of holy water. They all found their mark, turning the fifty something year old man, dressed in a suit and a bowler hat, carrying an umbrella, into a pool of water that turned to vapor that rose in the sky until it could no longer be seen. In his best John Wayne voice he said, "Well, I tell you, Pilgrim, this gun works pretty good against these ghosts."

Jason fell to the sand laughing like a mad man. When he recovered from his jag, he stood up. "Man that was very cool. The job shouldn't be too hard." He had no idea how wrong he would be.

2

They all arrived at the southern tip of the island. It was mostly sand with a few clumps of vegetation scattered about. They stood side by side and began walking north, searching the sand and the shrubbery carefully, not wanting to miss a hiding ghost.

Bernadette was the first one to score, taking out seven ghosts lying flat on their backs. They were all dressed in desert camouflage and she was momentarily shaken that she had to shoot dead military men-oops, make that four men and three women-but it was the only way they could move on and not haunt people on earth. She pulled the trigger and didn't let go, moving it back and forth, spraying a large amount of water bullets. The spirits took hits in many areas of their former bodies, dissolving rapidly, the vapor moving upwards. She didn't know why, but she felt nauseous, as though she killed living people. She had to reach deep inside and pull out a bucket full of faith, finally satisfied that she was doing something very important. She pulled the water bottle from a pocket and filled her squirt gun to the top. As she recapped the bottle, it refilled itself.

She took a sip of water from one of the bottles that survived the trip from the boat to the shore and wiped sweat from her brow. It was pretty hot and she figured it might get even hotter late this afternoon. It was hard for her to adjust to the weather after all those years of working nights on the carrier and then spending most days behind closed doors, venturing out only after the sun set on most days. The warmth felt good on her skin; skin that she loved looking at every chance she got and she was so happy with what God had done for her. She wished that someday everyone would have an opportunity to thank Him for something and become faithful. She knew too many people who had no faith at all and she just felt they were missing out on something very special.

Kyle saw her looking toward him and he gave her a thumbs up. He turned back toward the area in front of him and slowly moved his head from side to side and from near to far, looking for anything out of the ordinary. He thought searching for ghosts was probably the most fun thing he had ever done in his life so far. Sure, as a kid, he did some crazy things like bungee jumping off bridges, swimming in quarries, and driving cars as fast as he could, but doing this, being able to serve in something this huge, was the biggest kick so far. He had no problem shooting these ghosts because they would finally be free of their earthly constraints. He fervently hoped that Heaven would be a better place, as he heard so many people say after someone died. Suddenly, about ten yards in front of him and slightly to the left he saw a group of about fifteen lost souls. They had been kneeling, as if in prayer. *Do ghosts pray?* They stood up and held hands, walking toward him. He raised his weapon and fired one water bullet, wanting to send each ghost home one at a time. The bullet struck the ghost on the far right, and like dominoes, they dissolved one after another. A huge cloud of water vapor rose toward the Lord's home and he learned that more than one could be sent to Heaven or Hell with just one shot. He wanted to see if more than one could be sent home if they were in a line, one behind the other, without having contact. He smiled and started moving forward again.

Sam and Sammy were checking out a large area of vegetation and they weren't sure if they would be able to walk through it.

"Sam, I have an idea."

"Okay, Sis. Go for it."

She stood at the edge of the greenery and shouted. "We would appreciate if you all would come out here instead of us having to hunt you down. Many of you, perhaps all of you, are going to wind up in Heaven, so why don't you make it easy for yourselves."

They waited for five minutes and receiving no response were ready to start walking through when three ghosts passed through the plants and stood near them on the sand.

The two men and a boy appeared to have lived back in the seventeen hundreds based on the clothing they wore and the tri-cornered hats on their heads. They looked like regular people because their outfits weren't anything special, made of very coarse material.

"What is going to happen to us? We were roaming around Trenton, New Jersey, and then suddenly we were transported here. All I remember is something like a tunnel and as we were pushed through, we saw many, many ghosts. Some of the clothing they wore was quite shocking and I figured they lived during this age instead of back when we were alive." The older looking man had spoken for the threesome.

"You have been sent here by God and it is our job to shoot you with holy water. After the bullet enters your body, you will dissolve and the vapor will rise or get sucked into the sand, depending on where you are going to go."

The spirit smiled and nodded. "Thank you, Miss. My brother, his son and I thought we would be trapped here forever. Eternity is a long time and just wandering the earth is not the most appealing way to spend it. I believe we were good Christians so I hope we will be sent to Heaven. Please do what you need to do. We are anxious to see what is on the other side and hope to meet family members that passed a long time ago."

"Can I ask why you three have been earthbound so long?"

"That is an interesting question. We were in a small boat traveling from Philadelphia to Trenton and we hit something with the boat. It broke up rather quickly and I don't think we had the opportunity to talk to God one last time. We were too interested in staying alive until the weight of our clothing took us to the bottom. We grasped hands with one another and died in that freezing river. It was sad that Jonathan had to perish because he was only eleven."

"Thank you for sharing your story," Sammy said as she raised her squirt gun and fired three water bullets.

The water vapor rose and she was greatly relieved that they were indeed going to Heaven. She hoped they would meet up with their family and friends.

As the twelve ghost hunters pushed northward, the sun dropped lower and lower in the sky. They could see the end of the island and figured they had about a half hour of good light left. The ghosts would have been impossible to see had it not been for the special glasses they wore, and surprisingly, as it got darker, the glasses seemed to draw in and reflect all the available daylight.

Within fifteen minutes every visible ghost on the island had been dispatched.

Back at camp, Rick and Denise rebuilt the fire and by the time the sun set in a blaze of reds and yellows, they had all eaten the sandwiches that miraculously appeared in a cooler near the fire pit.

Darrell said, "I took the liberty of phoning a friend in Wilmington. He went to a deli and had all these fine goodies made up for us. I saw he also took the initiative to grace us with a cooler full of cold beer. Life should be pretty good tonight. I'm sure interested in the count for today. Every ghost that I sent home worked its way heavenward. I got six hundred and eighty three confirmed kills." He smiled because it just made it easier to call the spirits they got kills.

Bernie set up a spreadsheet on her iPhone and after entering everyone's names and their 'kills' she totaled it up. "I guess we had a pretty good day, sending four thousand thirty seven souls heavenward and none to Satan's domain. My gut tells me there are many out there that will fight us tooth and nail not to go, so I think we should get a good night's sleep and get an early start in the morning."

It was determined that the four women would take the tents and the men would just sleep on the sand. There were a couple of blankets which were given to Bill and Aaron because they were the oldest of the group. The two elder statesmen of the group took some good natured kidding about their ages, but they really did appreciate the additional warmth from the blankets.

By nine-thirty, everyone was asleep under the black night with few stars.

Monday, July 14th, 2014
Masonboro Island

From Darkness

They slept, deeply breathing, relaxing the activity of the day away. There was some soft snoring from three people, and if anybody would have been awake, they would have heard some coughing as well. The night air was cool, the wind coming from off the ocean, keeping the humidity at bay. In the nineties today and much the same for tomorrow.

Several hours later, like a stiff breeze rustling through the still air, hundreds of malevolent spirits descended upon the twelve sleeping humans. Many of them hovered above the inert bodies, so close they nearly became a part of them, watching the rise and fall of their chests, nearly able to feel the warmth coming from their mouths and noses. Not only were those on the beach being subjected to this paranormal invasion of their privacy, but the four women inside the tents were also being inspected.

Each spirit attempted to work its way inside a person, but none of them could do so. It was almost as if they were being blocked by a force stronger than them. Numerous efforts resulted in the same end. None of the humans were susceptible to possession and that would ruin the plan these wicked spirits had formulated. They managed to avoid detection all day, but they knew that if they didn't accomplish their mission, all would be lost.

One human, even through closed eyes, could see Satan's translucent troops attempting to permeate their evil deeds on what would soon be holy ground. Inside the human, God smiled knowing that soon the dark ghosts would be trapped there and annihilated by His soldiers; all hand-picked for this mission.

When God was certain that all the evil spirits on the island were gathered on the beach, He stood up, crying out, "Satan, your minions will be eradicated and sent to Hell, never to walk the earth and harm my people ever again." God waved the human's arms and an invisible dome dropped from the sky, effectively trapping all inside. Angels fluttered high above the sand, denying any ghost the opportunity to try to break through the Heavenly membrane placed there by the Creator of all and everything.

With another wave of his hands, God filled the dome with light, light that no one on the outside would be able to see. The immediate brightness awakened the remainder of the twelve, even after God withdrew from the body He had been using. It was now time for the humans to save their world, joining in the great battle versus the forces of Satan.

To Light

1

When Jason opened his eyes, he screamed, looking into the face of the most horrible entity he had ever seen, including the images of the soldiers he fought with in Afghanistan. She was probably once a beautiful woman, but now she had bulging veins in her face, red with blood. Her eyes were scarlet and green drool, the color of pea soup, flowed from her open mouth. Her mouth was filled with blackened teeth, maggots crawling out and dropping on Jason's chest. He tried to brush them off, but there was an unending supply. He heard her laugh, a cackling, and screeching sound, unlike anything he had ever heard. When she tilted her head closer to him, the awful, foul smelling drool dripped into his open mouth and he nearly gagged.

Hands like the talons of a hawk slashed out at his face, cutting ribbon like scratches on his face and his arms when he tried to block her attack. She laughed again, saying, "Human, you cannot defeat me, for I have the power of the Son of Perdition as my strength. Your God is weak and will be beaten, giving us the earth for our dominion." She sniggered again, throwing her head back and forth and from side to side, spewing more drool and maggots all over him, reaching out with her deformed hands locking them around his neck, then leaning in to kiss him, sliding her rotting tongue between his lips. Though sickened, he managed to find his squirt gun and when he stuck the barrel in her stomach and pulled the trigger, her eyes grew wide and she emitted a scream of unimaginable volume, causing him to wince as the unholy sound pierced through his ears and into his brain.

The demon ghost was shaken, but the bullet of holy water was not enough to put her into the ground forever and she tried to wrestle it from his grasp. She was unbelievably strong, but he was able to pull and hold the trigger, sending many water bullets into her body.

For a moment, he thought she was going to recover, and then she just suddenly dissolved, soaking him to the skin.

He stood up and shook, never wanting to experience the likes of that again, but only moments passed by before he was under attack again by four ghosts, all as horrible as the first one. He raised his weapon and began to fire.

2

Inside the two tents, the four women were being accosted by numerous ghosts. Though they were not as vicious as the ones now attacking Jason, they were formidable foes. Maura and Mandy managed to elude them and scamper from the tent, seeing all the men engaged in battle with all kinds of ghosts. There were men, women, and children all trying to take everyone down, and as fast as they attacked, they were shot down, dissolving into the sand, creating black spots.

Maura dropped her squirt gun and when she reached down to pick it up, she was hit by three ghosts and tossed backward, tumbling twice before she was able to regain her footing again. She raised her gun and looked for targets, but there were none in range. She saw Molly, Sammy and Denise come out from the tents; they seemed shook up, but with no ghosts near them, Maura figured they had taken care of business and sent their attackers packing.

She saw them looking at her with fright in their eyes, pointing and shouting for her to look out behind her. A moment later she had the wind knocked out of her, and found herself tumbling on the sand again, this time getting a mouthful. She coughed and spit most of the sand out and rolled over on her back. When she did this, two ghosts landed on her and it seemed like they were attempting to enter her body. She turned her gun on them and shot them down like dogs, adding two more black spots to the sand.

When she caught her breath and stood up, she saw the girls were in trouble, getting hammered by a dozen or more ghosts. She quickly rushed to their aid and within ten minutes the four of them dispatched all those spirits. The sand was nearly a sea of black, as the spots were close enough to link together. Yet when she searched the sky, there were just more and more of them, fighting like hell to not be sent to Hell. At this point, Maura didn't know if the twelve of them would be able to eradicate all of Satan's minions, but she wasn't going to go down without giving them the best fight of her life.

Just when she was ready to fire again, three ghosts knocked her backwards into her tent. One followed her inside.

3

Bill and Aaron were under attack by a large number of ghosts. Because of their ages, they were getting beat up badly. Talon scratches were all over their bodies and faces and they each lost a fair amount of blood.

Bill wondered how human spirits could change to unspeakably hideous creatures, capable of causing bodily damage to living beings because this never came up in any of the books he had read about ghosts. This was definitely not in his pay grade, but he was in for the long haul and no matter what happened to him, he would take out as many of them as he could.

Aaron had five ghosts clinging to him. He was able to shoot three and send them to Hell, but the other two just would not give up. "Bill, how about a little hand over here." He screamed to his new friend.

Bill evaded a spirit coming at him head on. He spun out of the way and then shot her as she turned around to come back for more. Before she dissolved she spat at him and his arm momentarily burned as though fire touched his skin. He shook away the pain and ran toward Aaron, firing holy water bullets as quickly as possible. He shot three that were clinging to Aaron, but it took numerous shots to put them down. Some of these bastards were pretty strong and capable of enduring several shots of holy water. He had to take some time to reload after that.

After dispatching those two repugnant ghosts, the two oldest fighters raced toward the ocean, seeing Sam, Sammy, Denise and Rick being pummeled by at least thirty disgusting former humans. This group was comprised of mainly women and children, but they were tough and dodged numerous shots.

4

Maura crawled out from the tent, a little dazed, but other than that she seemed okay to those who looked her way. She stood up and searched for her three friends. When she saw them in the heat of battle with countless spirits, she hurried over, but, she was not there to help.

A ghost had managed to possess her and the spirit forced her to grab Jason's nine millimeter pistol with a full magazine of nineteen rounds. Jason never went away without his weapon, but he also hoped to God he would never have to use it.

She raced toward Jason first and he never saw her coming. She raised the pistol and fired three rounds point blank into the back of his head. His face disintegrated as blood, bone and flesh spread out catching Darrell and Molly totally by surprise.

Mandy was fast, but not fast enough as a bullet tore into her shoulder, spinning her around, taking her to the ground screaming in pain. She couldn't believe what was happening and she was certain she was going to die as Maura leveled the gun at her again. She saw Maura's red eyes and when her mouth opened, spittle spewed out. Just before she fired, Darrell leapt at her, probably hoping to disarm her, but Maura caught his movement and turned the weapon on him, catching him with four rounds. One tore into his face, one took his left hand clean off at the wrist. Two hit him in the chest and he fell like a sack of garbage. He was dead.

Maura turned back to Mandy, who was pleading for her life. Mandy saw a glimmer of something human again. That moment was all Maura needed to say "Goodbye, Mandy", and turn the weapon on herself, pulling the trigger and not letting go as she danced with the impact of each bullet.

The spirit inside Maura exited her body and Mandy took him out with six shots of holy water.

5

The rest of the team was extremely busy keeping the wicked ghosts off of each other and as the sun peeked over the horizon, red waves of light dancing off the surface of the barrier, the men and one women left fighting were given assistance by the angels God had sent. Between human ingenuity and the power of almighty God, the remainder of Satan's ghostly sycophants, were sent to Hell. Most of the sand inside the dome had been blackened by their departures and it would be several weeks before no signs of a struggle would be gone.

The team all pitched in to make Mandy comfortable until she could get medical help. However, by the time the sun had fully risen, turning the sky a gorgeous blue, her wounds were healed. All the people who had sustained injures were also fully mended.

Rick and Sam covered the bodies of Jason, Darrell and Maura and then waited for what was to come next.

Food and water were on everyone's minds. They rifled through the coolers, drinking up whatever was left and there were some chips and pretzels remaining, so that was all they had to tide them over until they were taken off the island.

6

Later that morning, after everyone, except Bill and Aaron, took a nap, Bill cried out, "Hey guys, there's a boat on the horizon and I think it's coming this way.

The team stood up and they all waved as several inflatable rafts were coming toward shore.

Minutes later, they were all on board the yacht they had been on the other night, renewing their short friendships with the Jarous family; Todd, Cyndee and David.

After introducing Mandy to them and engaging in some small talk, the team was led to a dining area where there was food of all kinds for them to eat and lots of coffee, water, soda, beer and wine.

When the team was sated, they were requested to come up to the deck. They took seats wondering what was going to happen now and out of nowhere George and Hannah appeared.

Hannah smiled that sweet ten year old child smile at them; her love for them washed over each and every person on that boat and the people loved her just as much at that very moment.

George, dressed in white pants, a red shirt, a blue blazer, white tennis shoes, red socks and a white fedora with a red white and blue checked band also smiled. His eyes were hard to see through his thick lenses and through the plume of smoke from the large cigar he was smoking.

"Hannah and I do love big entrances, so we hope we dazzled you. After all, not everyone gets the opportunity to see one of the faces of God, do they?"

When everyone nodded and chuckled, he bowed smartly. "I want to thank you for your service to My Kingdom. I am saddened by the fact that Satan took three lives, but rest assured, he did not get their souls. They were good people but Maura just wasn't quite strong enough to fight *his* soldiers. I regret that I could not save them. I am not going to take up much more of your time because I know you are all anxious to get home to your families and friends so I will be brief."

"This mission was your first of many, if you choose to serve, that is. I will not force anyone against his or her will, and the gifts you have been given will not be taken from any one of you. I know you have many questions and in due time they will be answered, when we meet again. Everything that has occurred will never be shared with the rest of the world because I don't want any kind of panic. People have enough to worry about today. My only request is that you all seek out non-believers and talk with them. Perhaps you will be rewarded; perhaps not."

"Hannah and I will be leaving in a moment but rest assured we will never leave you. Thank you again for your service to God." He raised both hands and said, "Go in peace. Serve God."

With that said, He and Hannah disappeared and the boat filled with believers headed back to Wrightsville.

Aftermath

Rick and Denise

The morning sun was bright. The slight breeze coming off the Cape Fear River made the air feel a bit cooler than the actual temperature of eighty-one degrees. The high was supposed to be close to ninety and the humidity would become oppressive by mid-afternoon.

The Riverfront Farmer's Market was bustling with crowds of locals and tourists looking for good deals. The many scents of fresh cut and potted flowers, various foods cooking, candles, and a potpourri of freshly baked breads, pies, cakes and other sundry treats filled Rick Conlen's nostrils. His sense of smell was not quite as sharp as it had been when he had been sightless, but his nose still worked pretty well. The aroma of cinnamon really stood out and he followed his nose to a stand with hot cinnamon buns, glazed icing pooling around the circumference of each one.

His girlfriend, soon to be fiancée, although she didn't know it yet, was watching a folk artist strumming a guitar and singing "If I Had A Hammer." His voice was so pleasant and she was lost in the music until a warm cinnamon bun appeared in front of her face. Without any hesitation, she tore into it ravenously, nearly taking two of his fingers along.

"Watch it, woman. I might need them sometime yet in this life." He came around to her side and handed her the rest of the bun as he bit into the one he carried in his other hand. He listened as he chewed. "That guy's pretty good, isn't he?"

She nodded as she chewed. With half a mouthful she said. "Yeah, he is, Rick. I've been listening to him for a little while now. I took one of his cards after I put five bucks in his basket. I think he'll do pretty well today. A bunch of people have given him money so far and he probably has a lot of time left to sing. Let's take a walk."

They strolled, hand in sticky hand, up to the boardwalk along the river and stood for quite some time looking across the river at the battleship North Carolina. They could see people walking on the deck and climbing around the big guns.

"Gosh, it seems like forever since we sent all those earthbound spirits on their way to Heaven or Hell but it hasn't even been two weeks yet." Rick said, turning his head toward Denise.

She smiled. "I am still amazed by what were able to accomplish in such a short period of time but it is still so sad that Maura, Jason and Darrell died on that island. I actually thought we would all survive even battling those malevolent spirits. Some of them were really tough to eliminate."

"Yeah. I talked to Bill and Aaron for quite some time on the boat heading back to Wrightsville that day. For their ages, they really showed a lot of stamina and nerve. I think a lot of the Hellbound spirits attacked them figuring that they'd be easy to possess because they were so much older than the rest of us. I was really proud of them...everyone, though, I was so proud of everyone."

"What do you think George and Hannah will have us do next? It is easier to call him George than calling him God. For our Lord to come to earth in the guise of a well-known human was pretty awesome. Hannah was great as well. She was a feisty little ten year old girl."

"That is so true, honey. She certainly didn't take any crap from any of us. I wish she could hang out with us all the time, but I imagine she has a large number of assignments to take care of. Lots of people need help getting in touch with God again, and she gives one an awfully good nudge."

Rick looked down toward the water, leaning over the railing a little because something caught his attention. He didn't see anything unusual, but suddenly the hair on the back of his neck stood up and he felt himself being pulled over the railing until he fell into the river.

Denise screamed, drawing the attention of several people nearby. "Help us, please. My boyfriend fell into the river." All she saw was him falling, not being pulled, the short distance into the water.

Bill and Larry

Bill rang the doorbell and waited for someone to answer. He had just completed his first week of training with

Stevens Services and at the end of the shift yesterday there was an interoffice envelope in his mailbox. He had broken the seal, opened it and read the note.

Bill, my wife, Peggy and I would enjoy the pleasure of your company for breakfast tomorrow morning at our home. Please arrive around 8 AM and wear your Vietnam Veterans cap.

He touched the brim of his cap with his right hand, almost saluting, and then he turned around to look at the view from the top of the hill. Larry's house was at the highest point and from the front of the house, Bill saw the great battleship North Carolina in the distance. It was almost hard to fathom that less than two weeks ago, he and his eight new friends had ridded the ship of all its earthbound spirits. Sometimes it seemed like a dream, but it had been all so real.

The door opened and Bill turned around, seeing Larry, wearing a similar cap, smiling from ear to ear. He was dressed in black Bermuda shorts, sandals and a red St. Louis Cardinals t-shirt. His white beard and hair had been recently cut. He appeared to be in pretty good shape, even with a little belly going on.

"Bill, it was so good of you to come. Please step inside and you can join the others on the back patio. Breakfast will be served presently. I have to run upstairs to get Peggy in gear. She has never been a morning person and she has a tendency to dawdle at times. We'll join you in a few minutes."

"Thanks, Larry. This is something I never expected. Just letting me work for you is more than enough...." Tears formed in the corners of his eyes and he wiped them.

Larry hugged him. "Bill, you are going to be a real asset to my company. Your training has progressed even faster than with some of my younger men and women and you have a knack for making our clients happy. I've had several calls already. But enough about work, please go out and join the others and we'll talk later." He turned and walked up the stairs.

When Bill walked out to the patio he saw at least a dozen men and women of various ages, all sporting caps proclaiming their service and their conflict. He was given a nametag, which he pinned to his sport shirt. Everyone else was wearing logo t-shirts, but he didn't feel out of place, seeing their smiles. He was handed a cup of coffee and then he shook hands with everyone there; of course, the Vietnam vets hugged him, because they were brothers from a different time.

They sat down on every available seat, after loading their plates with eggs, meats, potatoes, grits, fruit, toast, and muffins. Also being served was SOS-shit on a shingle, which was cream chipped beef, usually ladled over toast, hot and cold cereals, juices-both vegetable and fruit, and that most maligned meat, Spam.

As they ate and chatted amongst themselves, Bill saw Larry and Peggy walk hand in hand onto the patio. She was radiant, wearing a yellow sun dress, white sandals and sunglasses. He figured she and Larry were probably early to mid-sixties. Although his hair was white, Larry could have passed for mid-fifties and Peggy appeared to be even younger, he thought.

The host and hostess filled their plates and sat down at a couple of empty chairs. They ate with gusto and after they finished, the dirty dishes cleared and pastries placed on the long table, more coffee was served. Larry stood up and said, Even though I see many of you at work, this breakfast is somewhat special because this is Bill's first time. He doesn't know what you all know, so I guess I should fill him in. Bill, could you please come stand beside me?"

Bill stood up and joined his boss, shaking his hand, and then turning toward the remainder of the guests, and then he turned toward Larry.

"Bill, I've known about you since that morning at breakfast. When I handed you my business card, my hand touched yours and I was able to 'see' what you are. You are one of God's angels, even though you may not be quite aware of that."

Bill's forehead furrowed, not even comprehending what Larry was talking about.

Larry put his hands on Bill's shoulders and stared deeply into his eyes. "Think back to all the times you had near misses with cars, drinking, Vietnam, and living on the street. There are more incidences where God gave you a push in the right direction, saving you for bigger things. I don't know if you have done what God has groomed you for, but we are all Christians here and just to have you in our midst is more rewarding than you could even imagine. My guess is that God wants you to live out your life and touch more people. I think the best way for that to happen is to assign you as my liaison, sending you out to all my franchises and spreading the Good News of God."

Bill spoke to his new friends. "I don't think I am one of God's angels, but I believe I would certainly enjoy being His ambassador for this company. I am honored, especially after the difficult life I have had. Thanks again, and I will try to make everyone proud of me and of this company."

After some small talk, Bill was ready to go. Larry escorted him to the front door and said, "On Monday we'll get started on your new position. Bless you, Bill."

As Bill walked toward his car, he remembered when he had a feeling of extraordinary strength that final day on Masonboro Island, battling all those malevolent spirits. He had a lot of thinking to do, but perhaps Larry did have second sight and everything he said was true. He smiled and held his head higher than he had in many years.

Aaron

1

When Aaron arrived back in Hellertown ten days ago, he walked into his house and saw that nothing was out of place. Everything was put back exactly where it belonged and he still had trouble believing what he had seen and all that he did in North Carolina. He stood in the kitchen and his hands were shaking so badly that his entire body began to spasm. Although there was no pain, the trembling he was experiencing could have even been worse than the agony of physical wounds.

During his time in North Carolina, he called Cynthia often, but he was never able to get ahold of her, leaving countless messages. He heard his phone ring and answered it. "Hi, honey. How are you doing?' he asked.

"Don't you honey me, Aaron. I've called you at least twenty times since Friday and you never answered, nor returned any of my calls. Were you at the casino all the time I was gone or were you fooling around on me, like you did fifteen years ago?"

"Neither, Cyn. I was in North Carolina battling ghosts. You should have seen what they did in our house. I took pictures and when you get home, I'll show you what was going on."

"Really!" she exclaimed, her voice dripping with sarcasm. "You can't come up with something better than total bullshit. I'll be home this afternoon and you better have a damn good explanation for what you've been up to." She ended the conversation, not even allowing him to answer.

He checked his phone and saw all the pictures he took. When he checked his outgoing call record, his calls to Cynthia were all there, as were all her calls to him. Yet when he checked his call lists while he was away, there were no recent calls from her displayed. He thought that rather curious, but when she was home, he'd show her the evidence and then all would be right again. He also hoped that she racked up some new customers and distributors.

2

Cynthia Pammer parked the car and hurried inside, with fire in her eyes.

She loudly called out, "Aaron, where are you? I want to see you this instant."

He came from the kitchen, meeting her in the living room. He carried two bottles of beer and handed her one. "Let's sit down and talk, honey."

When he sat, she continued to stand, taking a couple of healthy swallows of beer. "So, are you ready to tell me where the hell you were these past five days and why   I   couldn't   contact   you?"

He looked up at her. "Please sit down. I want to

show you some pictures that will prove everything I told you is true."

Reluctantly she sat down, leaving a foot of space between them. She took his phone and started scrolling through his pictures. Seeing nothing new, she handed the phone back. "Sorry, Aaron, there are no pictures of ghosts or anything that can get you off the hook with me."

He scrolled though the pictures and every one was there. He held the phone while she looked again.

She sat straight up as he showed her each and every picture, including the ones he took on the North Carolina and Masonboro Island. Her eyes drank in all the photos but she kept shaking her head in disbelief. "How could these pictures be visible now? They weren't when I held the phone."

He shrugged his shoulders. "The only thing I can think of is that the only way anyone can see these pictures is if I am holding the phone."

She slid next to him and said, "I am so sorry, honey, for not believing you. I want to hear the whole story about your adventure."

When he finished, about an hour and a half later, she had become a believer and was ready to start going back to church services after too many years away.

Five months later, Aaron was able to transfer all the pictures to the pages of his journal. It was published two months after that, converting many non-believers back to Christ.

Mandy

She'd been alone for nearly two weeks and the pain in her heart for her husband and her two dearest friends would take a long time to subside.

The group had determined that it would be better to bury them at sea, claiming that they had died in a boating accident.

Mandy didn't know how that would go over, because how could she convince friends and families without newspaper accountings, death certificates, coroner's reports, and the fact that she was still alive. George told her that no questions would be asked and the reports unneeded. She wasn't sure she could believe that, but in the scheme of things, anything was possible.

About a week ago, she brought in the mail and saw there was a letter from a film company in New York. They wanted to meet with Darrell and discuss a contract to make a movie based on his paranormal novel, 'Unknown'. There was also a phone number for him to call, so she called and told them that Darrell was dead. After offering condolences, Mandy was told that they would still like to make this movie and that she would receive a one-hundred thousand dollar bonus and she would receive a percentage of the profits. Mandy said she would talk it over with her attorney and get back to them. Next week she was to meet with the filmmakers in New York where she would sign the contract and meet the screenwriters. The movie was scheduled to go into production in February of 2015. Most filming would be done in Wilmington, North Carolina.

She was so happy that so many people would be able to see a screen adaptation of Darrell's highest selling book and she was looking forward to visiting North Carolina again.

Sam and Sammy

On the way home from their adventure, Sam called Pastor Johansson and put the phone on speaker, so Sammy could listen and talk.

"Hello, this is Pastor Johansson", the voice on the other end said.

"Pastor this is Sam Staunton. I'm driving back from North Carolina with my sister, Samantha, and we wanted to give you a call."

"It's good to hear from you, Sam. It has been much too long since we had conversations. How are you, Samantha?"

"I'm fine, Pastor Mark. We have a lot to tell you when we get back, but Sam has something he wants to tell you now."

"Yes, I do have something I want to tell you. I have instructed our attorneys to give you whatever amount of money you need to keep all the church programs operational and any funds that will be needed for any necessary repairs. Our folks would have liked that we are doing this for our church. We expect to be home sometime tomorrow afternoon and if we could meet with you on Thursday or Friday, that would be great."

He opened his appointment book and scanned the two dates. "Thursday afternoon is clear. Would that be good for you both?"

Samantha saw Sam nod and she replied. "Yes, Pastor Mark. That would be fine."

"Splendid. I will see you both then in my office."

When they got together with him, they told the entire story of what had transpired in less than a week.

After digesting all that information, he said, "That is a remarkable story and it would probably work well in a paranormal novel. I'm sorry, but I just can't comprehend all you have told me. How would events of that magnitude go undiscovered? How could you see The Crucifixion on a video?

Sam was livid. He abruptly stood up and was just ready to lay into his pastor when he saw them standing behind the minister's chair. He sat down quickly.

Pastor Mark became afraid when Sam stood up so quickly and then it seemed as though he was looking at something. Mark looked to both sides and then he smelled cigar smoke. He swiveled his chair one hundred and eighty degrees and saw George and Hannah standing there. He nodded, fully understanding Sam and Samantha's story because God was dressed in green and pink plaid knickers, a pink golf shirt and a cap that matched his short pants. He wore pink stockings and black golf shoes, hopefully without spikes. He was smoking a Cuban cigar, blowing out interlocking smoke rings.

He ran his left hand over the cigar and it vanished. "So sorry, Pastor Johansson. I wish I had never created tobacco. It is so addicting and my only vice, except for coffee, when I am here in human form. This is my associate, Hannah, of whom I believe you are aware."

"Oh my God!" Pastor Johansson uttered, without even realizing it.

"Yes, I am, but you may call me George. We've been here all this time listening to Sam and Samantha tell you of their experiences with earthbound ghosts. We've only appeared in the flesh, so to speak, to confirm their stories and to have you understand and believe. I know you have gone through many rocky times in your service to God, and trust Me, I will always be there for you. Now these two young people are going to give you monetary gifts the like you have never received before so the work of this church, both inside its walls and in all the nearby communities can continue and grow. Someday you may see Hannah or I again, but for now, we must leave." He looked toward the twins. "Keep doing the good things you are meant to do and someday, I will call upon you again for great deeds."

They disappeared and Pastor Mark turned toward his benefactors. "I am so sorry for disbelieving you both, but rest assured, it will never happen again. I promise you that.

The three shook hands and Sam and Sammy left to begin spreading God's love.

Bernadette

1

Aboard the plane, shortly after takeoff, when the seatbelt sign was turned off, Bernadette stared out the window at the clouds passing underneath the wings. Occasionally she could see patches of the earth, water, and some buildings from thirty-thousand feet.

She was anxious to get home and tell her parents about her jaunt to the east coast, especially since she had not been able to contact them by phone. She wondered if any of her new friends had the same experience, and she was pretty certain all of them had be placed in an electronic media blackout. There was nothing mentioned on any of the North Carolina news stations, nor print media, so it wasn't hard to believe that none of the ghost hunters could phone home.

When she sat in the waiting area, prior to boarding, she had been approached by several handsome men and two beautiful women, offering to buy her a preflight drink or two and though she was flattered, she turned them all down. She could understand the men approaching her, but having women make a play was something she had never even considered. Of course, she never dated anyone, so she really didn't know if she was straight or gay, but she figured she'd be able to find out once she was back home with the locals she knew.

Her seatmate, a middle-aged, balding, Hispanic man, made a pass at her the moment she was seated and she put him in his place toot sweet. It was going to be a long flight with no conversation and if it got weird at any point, she would simply request a seat change, since the plane was only about two- thirds full.

As the plane soared westward, she became uncomfortable; something didn't feel right and she was concerned that there could be a mechanical problem, but she wasn't sure what to say to a flight attendant. Planes shook all the time, but this shaking just seemed abnormal. Something made her open her laptop and type a couple of words in the search bar. She got a large number of hits for the question she posed and when a male flight attendant was beside her seatmate, she said, "Excuse me, but something doesn't feel right with the way the plane is handling and I think I found out why." She handed him the laptop and after he read for a few moments, he hustled toward the front of the aircraft but she could no longer see what he was doing. He did turn a little white, she thought.

2

Len Burmeister, a seven year veteran flight attendant saw what she was talking about and he knew he had to see the captain immediately. Perhaps the problem could be fixed in mid-flight, but he feared that they would have to land as soon as possible and go over the aircraft with a fine tooth comb.

He punched in the key code and opened the door. After he was in the cockpit, he closed the door and showed the captain Bernadette's laptop and what she had found.

After reading the short article and seeing the video, he said, "Who gave this information to you?"

"It was a young lady sitting in economy and she was adamant that I show this to you."

"Can you tell me what you saw on the screen before you brought the laptop to me?"

"I saw an article about wing stress and when I looked out the window over the wing, I could see movement that should not have been there."

"Did you also see a video?"

"No, I didn't. Did you?"

"Yes, I did. Please return the laptop to the young lady and offer my thanks. I will speak with her after we land."

Moments after Len returned the laptop to Bernadette, the captain spoke to the passengers.

"We are experiencing some minor problems and we are going to land in Chicago in ten minutes to have the plane checked out. We probably will be on the ground less than one hour and during that time, you will please remain seated with your seat belts on. Thank you."

3

Bernadette was happy to hear that the captain was going to land the plane shortly. Although Len was not allowed to see the video of the wing falling off and the plane crashing, what he read was enough to get the captain's attention. She looked out her window and could see the wing, shaking wildly, beginning to affect the passengers with what seemed to them like turbulence. About thirty seconds later, she smiled when she saw three angels hovering under the wing, keeping it from falling off and they landed safely.

"Miss, the captain would like you to come to the cockpit?" Len said.

When she arrived in the cockpit and Len was dismissed and the door closed the captain said, "How did you know the wing was going to fall off and what happened during those last few minutes before we landed. Nothing felt wrong with the plane for that time period?"

"Just a feeling, captain." She smiled. "I am a very religious person and I prayed that we land safely. I guess God answered that prayer for me."

He nodded. "My other question is how in the world did I see a video of what would happen to the plane if I wouldn't have landed? I saw the plane go down and explode on contact with the ground."

"Captain, the Lord works in mysterious ways. He wanted you to know what could happen and I have to believe that everyone on the plane is supposed to live; some or all of us have found favor with God and He has work for us to finish. Once I leave this cabin, you will not remember this conversation and both you and Len will not recall having seen the message and the video. When the plane is looked over by the mechanics, they will see the problem with the wing and repairs will be made immediately. In time, you will be contacted by God and He will give you an assignment. Have a glorious day."

When she left the cockpit and returned to her seat, she knew that the captain and his crew would have no memory of what had just transpired. Len and all the passengers who saw her going to the cockpit would have memory loss of that as well.

In less than an hour, the plane was back in the air and they landed in LA safely.

Kyle

Two days after he returned to San Antonio, Kyle went to the VA for his scheduled appointment.

When he walked through the door and into the reception area, jaws dropped and staff members stared at him in shock. They had never seen him walking, and in fact, his records showed that his spine had been severed and he would never walk again.

He checked in without offering any explanation and sat in the waiting area until he was called for his appointment.

After the nurse took his vitals and weighed him, she escorted him to the doctor's office where he waited for twenty minutes until Doctor Washburn stepped in, sending or answering a text, not seeing him out of his wheelchair until he looked toward him and promptly dropped his phone.

"Kyle, where is your wheelchair and who helped you in?"

Kyle stood, took four steps to his doctor and shook his hand. "Doc, you may or may not believe this but last Friday I was the recipient of a miracle and I will never be in a wheelchair again."

"You know what you are telling me is an impossibility because your cord was severed, of course."

He nodded. "You're probably going to want to order x-rays and you will see that my spine is perfect."

"Yes, I will need to see x-rays, and I believe you. There will be no evidence that your spine was ever severed. I honestly don't know how I am going to report this, but I'm certain that doctors the world over will want to examine you and attempt to come up with an answer of how you can be walking again. Severed spinal cords do not repair themselves and there is no way on earth any doctor has the ability to surgically repair it."

Kyle was taken to x-ray, but he refused to be taken there in a wheelchair. He would never sit in one again.

After he was subjected to many x-rays, he was escorted back to the Doctor Washburn's office. Soon afterward, Doctor Washburn arrived with the x-rays in hand and he showed them to Kyle.

"As I said, Kyle, there is nothing on these x-rays to show that your cord was ever cut. The good news and bad news about this is that your one-hundred percent disability will be taken away from you, but now you will be able to seek employment anywhere you choose, doing whatever you want to do."

Kyle said, "Well, losing that income is going to pose some problems until I find a job, but I have a little saved up, so I guess I'll be okay."

Doctor Washburn stood up and offered Kyle his hand. "Son, if you have any financial difficulties at all, please call me and I will help you with whatever you need. What do you think you would like to do with the rest of your life?"

"I had quite an experience last week and saw some things that I will never be able to explain, but with the knowledge I gained, I'm going to see if I can get a job as a tour guide at the Alamo. I'm also going to research the battle and write what I know will be a true account of what happened."

"Good luck, Kyle. I don't ever want to see you here again as a patient, but I do want us to keep in contact. I will look forward to your book because I had a distant relative who died there. I can loan you all the information I have collected over the years."

"Thanks, Doc. I will look forward to our meetings."

He walked out into the Texas sunshine, looking forward to the rest of the day and all the days to come.

Rick and Denise

Rick thought he saw someone pulling him over the railing, but the figure was nearly translucent. He realized it was a spirt, but all of the spirits were sent away and there were not supposed to be any left. Just before he hit the water, he took a deep breath and when he was under, he felt the hands around his neck, strangling him. He brought his hands up and grabbed his unseen attacker's invisible hands and after a short struggle, managed to pull them from his neck. He quickly turned around to see Cecil laughing at him in the murky river.

With his air running short, he quickly swam to the surface, sucking in a boatload of fresh oxygen. He bobbed around, looking up until he caught Denise's eye. "It's Cecil, honey." He felt the spirit pulling his legs, sending him underwater yet again.

Just before he went under, he saw Denise pull something from her purse, climb over the railing and dive in.

She hit the water and swam toward Rick, seeing Cecil pulling him further and further toward the bottom of the river. Denise was afraid that Cecil would be able to pull Rick all the way down into the muck and she would never find him.

Swimming downward with all the strength she could muster, she managed to put herself below the ghost and her boyfriend. In her hand was a squirt gun.

Denise closed in on the malevolent spirit and fired three holy water bullets into his back.

Cecil let go of Rick and turned on Denise. The shots didn't disintegrate him and she was now afraid that both she and Rick would drown in the muddy water of the Cape Fear River.

Rick saw Cecil going for Denise and he kicked his legs hard, laying his hands on her attacker. Rick felt a surge of energy, almost as though someone else was helping him to subdue Cecil. Then he felt invisible hands on top of his. He knew an angel was with him but he still didn't know if Cecil could be destroyed before he took Denise's life. He saw the squirt gun fall from her hand and begin to float away. Fortunately, the weapon was floating toward him and he was able to grab it.

He turned and just kept squeezing the trigger, sending a jet of holy water into Cecil's body.

Rick saw the ghost squirm and then he saw Cecil smile and nod.

Cecil vanished and once he was gone, the angel also disappeared.

Rick and Denise swam upward and when their heads appeared, they were greeted with all the people standing around applauding.

After they were helped up to the boardwalk, they kissed passionately.

A thirty something man was walking by, carrying a drum. He yelled out, "Get a room."

Denise and Rick laughed and then strolled away.

70146501R00115

Made in the USA
Columbia, SC
05 May 2017